P9-APN-021

Child of the Holy Ghost

THE BASQUE SERIES

ROBERT LAXALT

Child of

UNIVERSITY OF NEVADA PRESS

the Holy

RENO : LAS VEGAS : LONDON

Ghost

Basque Series Editor: William A. Douglass

The paper used in this book meets the requirements of American National
Standard for Information Sciences—Permanence of Paper for Printed
Library Materials, ANSI Z39.48-1984. Binding materials were selected for
strength and durability.

Library of Congress Cataloging-in-Publication Data

Laxalt, Robert, 1923–

Child of the holy ghost / Robert Laxalt.

p.   cm. — (The Basque series)

ISBN 0-87417-196-2 (cloth : acid free paper)

1. Basque Americans—History—Fiction.   I. Title.   II. Series.

PS3562.A9525C48   1992

813'.54—dc20   92-7216

CIP

University of Nevada Press, Reno, Nevada 89557 USA

Design by Richard Hendel

Printed in the United States of America

2 4 6 8 9 7 5 3

For our children

Bruce, Monique, and Kristin

La beauté, c'est la vérité

O·N·E

1

I really hadn't wanted to go to the trouble of finding out about my mother. In the first place, that was not why I had come to the Basque Country to live. I had come to learn about the ways of the Basques in their ancestral villages. They happened to be my ancestral villages too, although I was an American born an ocean and a continent away.

I already knew about how immigrant Basques lived and thought in the United States, but there had always been something missing, and that something was how they lived and thought in their natural element. That was vital to understanding them.

In the second place, I didn't give a damn about the circumstances of her birth, which was exactly the way I had put it to my mother when she told me about it in one agonized torrent of words. Since it hurt her so much, I wanted to cut it off and never hear of it again. She was my mother, and that was the only important thing. The details did not bother me in the least.

Now, as unexpected as a lightning bolt I was forced to take the detour into my mother's past before I could go on with my work. The detour would be temporary and not interfere with my project, or so I told myself then.

What turned me off my intended course was an incident that happened in the Basque village where I had gone to live. My cousins Xavier and Adele took me to see an *amerikanoa,* that is, a Basque who had gone to America and managed to make and save enough money herding sheep to return to the Basque Country and buy a little farm.

When we were introduced, the *amerikanoa* shook my hand firmly in the American way. He was a stocky little man with black hair graying at the temples and decisive black eyebrows over penetrating eyes. He was not a man to be taken lightly, and I liked him instantly.

In the manner of the country, he invited us inside for a glass of sherry. Except for the routine questions about where he had herded sheep in the American West, I was content to listen and say nothing while my cousins visited with him. It was understood that I would return later to talk with him about his experiences in America and afterwards in the Basque Country.

Then, *not* in the manner of the country, he asked Xavier and Adele if I were their American cousin. I nodded, because it was a fact. But neither of my relatives nodded. With the perfect aplomb that comes from having prepared themselves for the question, Adele smiled as if the *amerikanoa* had said something preposterous. "No. He is merely an American friend."

When I recovered from that, it was to think, "Well, if that's the way they want it, it's all right with me." Another moment of dwelling on it showed me what her response truly meant.

I remembered an autumn afternoon when I was writing in my mother's sprawling old house in Nevada. In a few days, I was to leave for the Basque provinces of France, accompanying my father, Petya. He was going to his natal village to see a dying sister and what remained of his family after half a century as a sheepherder and livestock man in the American West.

My mother refused to go with him to see her own family and natal village for some reason that her rote response of "I am an American now" didn't explain. My father said that even so he would pay her respects to her family. That was his gallant way, but I understood later that it meant she had not told even *him* her secret.

Knowing that I would be hearing things, even though they were not totally revealing, and seeing family tombstones with names engraved on stone, she knew I would begin to wonder why her maiden name was different from that of her sisters. I would put two and two together without much effort and come up with the right answer.

So she had decided to wait until everyone else was away and she and I were in the big old house alone and then tell me her secret. It cost her terribly.

"Peter," she said when she came into the room where I was working. "Can I talk to you?"

When I turned my swivel chair around, I was astonished to see that her face was flushed, her fine features contorted, and her hands trembling. She was a woman who kept her reserve and composure no matter what.

Her confession poured out of her in a burst of unintelligible words, most of it in English but some of it in French, as though her mind had been living in two worlds at the same time. I remember the word *illé-gitime* because I had never heard it pronounced before. She repeated it time and again because, I suppose, it had been recorded indelibly on things like baptismal and school certificates and the passport she had been so careful never to let us see.

Whatever else she said slipped past me then, to return to memory in its proper time. I watched in dismay as this pillar of our family's strength began to disintegrate into fragments and then I got up quickly to take her in my arms. That was the second time I could remember doing that in my life. Our family is not given to touching. The first time was when I was going overseas in the war and a premonition had washed over me that I wouldn't be coming back.

"Mom! Mom! Do you think I give a damn?" I shouted at her, anything to stop her pain. "You're our mother and *this* is your country. We don't care about that Middle Ages nonsense over there!"

So my mother and I left it there. Though she asked me not to say anything to my brothers and sisters, I did tell my brothers. When I thought about it, I was not sure how my sisters would take it. My brothers shrugged it off the same way I had, the American way.

I did not dream then what havoc the fact of illegitimacy could wreak in the Old Country way. Though I had thrown it off flippantly, I had hit the nail on the head. It was Middle Ages stuff as surely and as horribly as witchcraft.

Soon after, when I went to France with my father, I did see the unexplained differences on names engraved on family tombstones. The
names were engraved in stone, all right, just to make sure relationships
were placed in their proper perspective. It rankled, but even then I
attached no importance to my mother's revelation.

But at this moment I was denied by my own blood kin in front of a
total stranger.

As for the *amerikanoa,* I could sense he had lived long enough in
the United States to learn how unimportant those things were in the
melting pot. The *amerikanoa* read the anger in my eyes and deliberately
posed the question, "Is your mother from this province?"

"My mother's maiden name was Maitia Garat," I said, spacing my
words for emphasis. She was born here in this village of Donibane and
the name of her house is Garat."

The *amerikanoa,* a little smile on his face, nodded in approval. "I
thought so," he said.

My cousins fled from the disaster. They did not speak to me all the
way back to the village inn where I had rented a room, and very little
afterwards. I came to regret that, because they were both accomplished
gossips and therefore sources of information. What they did not know
was that I was as coldly angry as they. More, even. I had made my
decision then and there to find out all there was to know about my
mother.

·   ·   ·   ·

My God, what a long time it took and what a hard time it was to get
anybody, even family, to tell me *anything.* It was as if it were unnatural
for a son to find out the simple truth surrounding his mother's birth.

These little villages guard their scandals fiercely. Their scandals are
precious to them, to be taken out and savored with relish, and *not* to
be shared with outsiders. They are the sole and exclusive property of
the village and its inhabitants, never to be revealed to a stranger. It took
a while for me to understand that not having been born there, I was a

stranger too, even though I was of blood, but finally I did. I even tried to feel charitable toward the villagers of Donibane.

When they saw I was determined and that I did know *something,* they began to talk. Cautiously and reluctantly at first, they began to build upon the knowledge I had accumulated. As the sum of my knowledge built, I had more to offer in trade. After that, there was no shutting them up, and the task became one of sorting the truth from the embroidery.

·   ·   ·   ·

How different it was in the province of my father in the high mountains of the Pyrenees. How little trouble it was to find out about *his* beginnings in the Old Country. They are called *Zubero* Basques there, and they, in their splendid isolation in the high mountains, are puzzled by the guile of the lowlanders in Basse Navarre, which was my mother's province. They are puzzled to the point that they do not consider the lowlanders to be Basques at all and come back from their infrequent journeys to the lowland shaking their heads in incomprehension at the way the lowlanders conduct themselves.

In this high province, a question honestly asked will earn an honest answer immediately, without any more importance attached to it than if someone had asked a question about the weather. Such accidents of youth as premature bedding and illegitimacy are of no moment. They are the facts of life and are accepted as that. The high mountain Basques tell the truth down to the last comma, and they are sticklers for accuracy.

Few of them leave their mountains to emigrate to the Americas, north or south. They love their ancient earth and surrender it only in extreme circumstance.

When they must leave, usually out of poverty, they carry their candor and their love of accuracy with them. That was the way it was with my father, Petya, in America. Any question I asked him about the early days on the western range or his beginnings in the Old Country got an answer. There was not the least attempt at evasion, even when we talked about shootouts with cattlemen whose names have gone down in history books as empire builders but who would rather forget about such embarrassing episodes as bushwhacking solitary sheepherders.

My father had learned his English on the open range in a day when the minds of men who inhabited it were uncluttered by books and radio and television. He could recall word for word a conversation he had heard fifty years ago, and every incident that he, at least, considered important. I can remember him and his brother, my uncle Joanes, arguing around the campfire about whether they began moving the sheep from winter range to summer range on May 10 or May 11. 1924.

2

Maitia was born a Child of the Holy Ghost. That was the way the saying went then, and one can still hear it in the remote pockets of Basse Navarre where language does not change quickly.

She did not become aware of the designation until well after she had started school in the village, and even then she did not comprehend what it meant. For a while, she imagined it to be a special sort of compliment having something to do with the fact that she loved God, went to vespers, and said her prayers every morning and night.

At that, there was a certain amount of charity involved. The word *bastard* could just as well have been used. I had lived in the Basque Country long enough to see how the lowland Basques delight in leavening their insults with a wry touch not unlike the stinger in a scorpion's tail.

They are sacrilegious with caution, since the expression after all applied first to the child Jesus. They never were able to swallow the story of the virgin birth.

They have never forgiven Saint Peter either. There are any number of stories about him in Basse Navarre, and he does not come off well in any of them. Take the one about a priest of doubtful morals who died and in due course had his confrontation with Saint Peter at the gates of Heaven. Saint Peter upbraided the priest for betraying his vows.

The priest flew into a perfect rage, crying, "Who are you to talk about betrayal? You denied Christ three times."

But these are little sacrileges, and they are the exclusive property of men. The village priests must look for satisfaction of their mission in Basque women, who, I have come to understand, put on a good show of being pious. The men have never pretended to piety. They go to Mass mainly as an excuse to sing, and afterwards to indulge in food and drink.

In the Basque way of doing things, the men perch on their benches segregated in balconies overlooking the nave of the church, where the women and children sit. The women sing the priest's part and the men sing the responses. The men's voices are properly restrained during the Ordinary of the Mass. But when the Basque Angelus comes up at the end, their voices are irreligiously lusty so that the little church seems actually to rock with sound.

Afterwards, the men bid goodbye to their wives and hurry to the bars and restaurants that abound near the village church. There, they drink and eat and sing until the middle of the afternoon. They feel no guilt about this, one and all justifying themselves with the timeworn excuse, "I have worked hard all week, and I have earned my cup." They feel no need to explain that their cup should have been measured in bottles.

The lowland Basques will deceive themselves that illegitimate children are welcomed with open arms into the family fold. This is taken to be proof of the generous nature of the Basques. The truth is that on most of the little farms sprinkled over every inch of valley land, helping hands are much in demand, and no one is going to get choosy about the manner of a birth when it comes to that.

The grandparents, who are usually saddled with the chore of raising illegitimate children, are fiercely protective of them and do not discriminate against them in such institutions as inheritance, although they have the legal right. As in most things Basque, tradition can often be stronger than the law.

Still, the family must bear the stigma on its respectability. Their neighbors will never let them forget it unto the third generation. When I learned that and saw it in practice, part of the riddle of my mother's obsession with respectability in America was revealed to me. I understood things I had wondered about vaguely before.

As for the girl who commits the indiscretion of mothering out of wedlock, there is no protection. She might as well be dead. Unless, that is, she is the eldest child and therefore the heiress to a substantial property. In that case, the practical nature of the Basques asserts itself and the unwed mother will have no shortage of suitors among the young men of poorer properties.

My grandmother, Jeanne, was an eldest child, and my mother in her turn also was. But as things turned out, it did my mother no good.

. . . .

In my mother's bedroom in the family home in Carson City, there was an oval photograph in gilt-edged framing of *her* mother, Jeanne Garat. The portrait had been blown up and tinted in the fashion of that time in America.

Jeanne was a slender girl with auburn hair pulled back to set off the delicate bones of her face. Her forehead was high and proud, her eyes gray and intelligent, and her nose so finely bridged and fragile that it seemed the pressure of a finger could crush it.

The photograph bore out what I heard from the old women of Donibane. In a country where pretty girls are commonplace, Jeanne was known for her extraordinary beauty, though some said she carried her head too high for their tastes.

Jeanne was the pride of the tiny *quartier* that lay only a mile from the main village of Donibane. From the time of the Romans, Donibane had been a capital of sorts for the Basque province of Basse Navarre in France. Since the village lay at the foot of the high Pyrenean pass into Spain, its cobblestone streets had known the tread of Caesar's legions, Visigoth barbarians, Moors, and the Grand Army of Napoleon. In fact, it was Napoleon's architect, Vauban, who had ordered the fortification of the village with immensely thick stone ramparts and an interior Citadel overlooking the valley. Now, the Citadel was an untenanted fortress with crumbling turrets, musty subterranean tunnels, blackened musket slits, and a surrounding moat long emptied of water and filled with a profusion of grass and flowers. It was a favorite meeting place for young lovers of the village.

Jeanne's parents were of an old and respected family, neither rich nor poor, but with a fine strong square house whose stone walls were whitewashed every year, shutters freshly painted in red, and blackened tiles on the roof that were replaced, when they surrendered to time, by new ones of bright earth colors.

The farmhouse still stands, and the carved keystone over the door still proclaims that the house had been built by a Nikolas Garat in 1454.

I am sure that another century will have no more effect upon it than the last five have. Now, as then, the farm possesses a flourishing vegetable garden; blonde cows give good milk and work as yoke oxen when there are heavy loads of hay and straw to be moved. Most importantly, they still bear good calves that can be sold for veal on village market days. Pigs and sheep and chickens mingle together over the verdant fields, and on the hillsides, venerable old vines yield grapes of reputation for the making of wine.

The *quartier* itself lies in a protected hollow bounded on one side by the River Nive and on the other by thick forests of beech, chestnut, and walnut trees, gnarled and mossy old oaks, and a veritable jungle of berry bushes that are communal property when picking season comes.

In Jeanne's time the property provided for the needs of the family. They were never without milk and vegetables and fruit. Glorious hams and bacons cured with red pepper and salt hung in abundance from oaken overhead beams in the kitchen and attic of the house. Trout could be had by a visit to the wire trap sunk in the river, and once in a while Jeanne's father, Garat, permitted the killing of a suckling pig or a lamb, instead of the usual chicken, for a feast-day dinner. Garat was sparing in this practice, however, because lambs and pigs and milk-fed calves for veal were the farm's main source of cash money on market day in the village.

In my time there, the matriarch of the farm domain known as the House of Garat was an old widow named Marie Ttipi. This is to say Little Marie, a designation used when there are two daughters of the same name in the family. She may have been diminutive when she was a child, but not when she grew to adulthood. She was tall and rangy, if that word can be used to describe a woman. Her gray hair was pulled back in a chignon, and the fine lines around her eyes always seemed to have a twinkle in them. The twinkle was genuine, because her attitude toward life was one of wise amusement. She was a Garat, too, the daughter of Jeanne's younger brother, Jean-Baptiste. The Garat homestead went to him just before my mother left for America. The true circumstances of that passing were not pretty, but I am convinced that Little Marie never knew the whole story.

Little Marie was the eldest daughter of Jean-Baptiste and the wife he finally took when his playing and drinking days were over. When her parents died, the property passed to Little Marie as eldest offspring. She accepted the responsibility with a shrug and the knowledge that running a farm would also mean much work for her and her husband and their growing brood. She had inherited nothing of her grandfather Garat's famous irascibility.

A curious thing happened in my first days in the village of Donibane. From the inn where I had taken up lodging, I had gotten directions and driven out to the House of Garat to say hello.

When I told Little Marie that I had rented a room in Donibane, she was genuinely irate. "But why don't you stay here?" she said. "This is your *home*."

I took that to be just a courtesy and nothing more, and used as an excuse the fact that I would be traveling almost constantly and didn't want to disrupt the ordered life of the farm. Later, I learned that she was serious about the farm being my *home* and asked her how and why that could be. She told me, amazed that I didn't know the ancient lineage of the farm. In this moment and in many moments afterwards, the twinkle would fade from Little Marie's eyes to be replaced by the furrowed brow and serious gaze of intense concentration. Watching her then, I knew she would never lie to me. I learned much of value from Little Marie.

I visited the farm often, sometimes to help her son Albert with the planting and haying but mostly to talk with Little Marie. Through the cold months of winter and early spring, she would place me beside the kitchen fireplace with its massive andirons of gray, polished steel and blackened cooking pot. It gave me an odd feeling of familiarity when I learned that my mother, her mother, Jeanne, and generations of my family had sat on the same straight-backed wooden bench.

·   ·   ·   ·

Once, we were talking about market day in the village of Donibane. Going to it was a ritual as entrenched as going to Mass and vespers on Sunday. But as far as my grandmother Jeanne had been concerned, another ritual always preceded it.

Garat had not been so blind as to ignore the allure that radiated from his daughter or to overlook the young men who responded to that allure. So it was that every Sunday night before Monday market day, Garat had lectured Jeanne on the importance of respectability.

"No woman—mother or daughter or cousin—escaped from those lectures," Little Marie told me. "They have been passed down to my generation verbatim. Every word is still stamped on my memory. 'A good reputation is worth more than a golden belt.' 'Tell me who your friends are, and I will tell you who you are.'"

The smile returned to Little Marie's face. "Then old Garat would shift the burden away from Jeanne by including himself," she said. He would say, "We are an old family and we are respected. I have to watch my conduct, too. If I got drunk and fell down, no one would ever let me forget it."

Market day in the village had really not changed much between then and my time. The Basque Country is suspicious of change, believing that it means disrupting an order that has been tested and proven.

On market day, Garat and his son, Jean-Baptiste, who was then four-teen, would rise early to hitch up the mule to a sturdy red cart for the hauling of calves or pigs or lambs to the livestock sale that made up the morning's activity. There, they would unload their animals in the Garats' time-honored pens positioned against the ramparts below the Citadel.

Morning was the men's time and the main street of the village was a panoply of black berets, coats of black and brown, and dark blue, loose-fitting pants worn over good trousers. Some men had hawklike noses and brooding eyes and blade faces. Others were burly Basques with deep chests, thick necks, and beetling brows, and all possessed a common denominator of strong hands into which the dirt of a lifetime of work in the fields had ground itself, leaving dark ravines in the flesh.

The livestock buyers in their gray smocks with pencil-filled pockets stalked past the pens with harangues of wit and sarcasm, feeling animals' backs with sure, knowing fingers and lifting their tails to look at the one place where disease cannot be concealed and where a calf who has tasted grass will be found out. In the end, the buyers nearly always won in their bartering, because they could tell at a glance who needed money.

The women of the *quartier* finished up their chores by noon and walked to Donibane for the afternoon market. By then, the men had retired to the restaurants and the bars and they would not be seen again until the market was done. The livestock pens had been replaced by fruit and vegetable vendors who catered to landless villagers and by the temporary stalls of itinerant gypsy merchants who moved from market day to market day in the scattered villages. The afternoon was mostly the farm women's time and they wandered the streets, visiting with each other and their friends among the village dwellers, and bought the things they could not raise—coffee, spices, and sugar, fish brought up from the seacoast, tobacco for their husbands, and, sparingly, clothes for the family.

Then, as in my time, they were rarely accompanied by their daughters, who preferred to walk to the village together in bright skirts and laced bodices, sandals and head scarves, holding hands and singing along the way. When they got to the village, they struck a more dignified pose for the benefit of the young men of the village and the country farms, from whom they would one day choose a husband that matched their station in life.

Circumstances being what they were, Jeanne had to give up casting covert glances at the groups of boys walking together through the throng of women. The reason for this was that her future had already been negotiated for and settled by her parents, Garat and his long-suffering wife. Jeanne was promised in marriage to an enterprising businessman named Labadiste. It was a fact of life known by everyone in the village.

So also was the story of Labadiste's rise to fortune. The example he set and the opportunities he created for himself were still being imitated in the village when I lived there.

Labadiste had been one of the rare young men of Donibane who had had a full measure of schooling. He had finished what the French call *lycée* and competed successfully for his bachelor's certificate in business. And after that, his pharmacist father had sent him for two years to business school in Bordeaux, a rich seaport and commercial town more famous for the wines of the region.

Labadiste was the first to see the opportunities in recruiting and exporting young Basques from impoverished farms, or those who by the accident of not being born the eldest child had no future in the Basque Country. In the latter instance, a young man could of course remain on the family farm in a role tantamount to servant, join the priesthood, or go to the village to serve a long and penniless apprenticeship to an artisan of some sort. They were the disinherited. It was no wonder that they chose instead to venture to the Americas to seek their fortune, whatever it turned out to be. Certainly they would be no worse off, even if fortune eluded them.

Some indeed came back with enough money to buy a plot of ground, build a house, and start their own family lineage. But even in this they suffered a loss. Once having left the Basque Country, they were never really regarded as Basque again and bore the name *amerikanoak*. Despite ten thousand years of being Basque, they had in a few years of absence become outsiders. Most of them were philosophical and sought the company of other *amerikanoak* with whom they could share experiences. Others tired of their stateless role and barbs such as, "Well, he may be rich now, but he came from nothing. I remember him when he went barefoot." Or, "He couldn't succeed here, so he had to go to America." The authors of these comments conveniently forgot, of course, that there was no way in God's world the *amerikanoak* could have succeeded if they had stayed home.

Those who grew tired of the subtle ostracism threw up their hands and went back to a New World where such distinctions did not apply, where rags to riches was the stuff of heroes and presidents.

In his own way, Labadiste had to bear his share of barbs. He was called a slave-trader, though never to his face. He would not have cared anyway. Being of a philosophical bent, he knew the strain of envy that runs through the Navarrese Basques and put it into proper perspective. A man had two choices. If he aspired to nothing, he would not be criticized. If he aspired to something, then he would be criticized. It was as simple as that. He chose the latter course and was not unhappy for it. And then there was always the salving balm of having swiftly become a rich man.

Labadiste had begun his exporting enterprise in human beings in a small office in Donibane. The difficulty of making long-range contacts with consular offices and steamship companies soon led him to the conclusion that he should have another office in the busy seacoast city of Bordeaux. So he went to Bordeaux and established his main base of operations there. From then on, his visits to his natal mountain village were only to see his family and to recruit strong young Basques to work in the Americas.

In time, he embellished upon his operation and bought a small hotel near the railroad station in Bordeaux. It was another in a long line of shrewd strokes. Why should someone else profit from the room and board his recruits needed in transition to foreign parts? All that his young men had to do was to walk with their clothes sacks from their farms to his little office in Donibane. From there, they would be put on the rickety little train to Bordeaux, met at the railway station, housed and fed in the hotel, put on the train to Paris and met there by a friend of Labadiste who would put them up in his own little Basque hotel, taken to Le Havre and put on the ship that would take them either to New York or to Buenos Aires in Argentina, met by another Basque who would put them up at another hotel, and finally transported to the North American ranch or Argentine *estancia* where they would spend some or all of their lives as sheepherders or gauchos. From beginning to end, Labadiste's young Basque men were led by the hand to their final destinations. No one could fault him for casting them adrift to find their own way. What they encountered when they got to where they were going was no longer his concern.

There was a minimum amount of risk involved in the total arrangement. Most times, the foreign employer of Labadiste's young men advanced to him their travel and living fare, and of course a healthy commission. Other times, Labadiste would advance the expense of passage to the young men himself. In either case, the young men would have to work a few years of their lives as indentured servants to reimburse their employers or Labadiste. The investment was not based as much on trust as it seemed. Labadiste was banking on the Basque passion for honoring debts, even if ten years went by in the process.

3

Under ordinary circumstances, Jeanne's standing as an eldest child and the prospective *héritière* of a prosperous farm, coupled with her striking beauty, made her the most eligible of young women. Labadiste could not have been the only young man to be attracted to her, but in his case, it was not for reasons of money. For him, whatever Jeanne would inherit meant nothing. By the time he was thirty, he was rich enough that he could have bought and sold her promised inheritance ten times.

In his own particular way, Labadiste was in love with Jeanne. That was the way the story went, but I suspect it was invented to justify the arrangement. From all his actions, one would have to be blind not to arrive at the conclusion that he was neither a passionate nor a romantic man.

Since Little Marie, unlike others, owed Labadiste nothing and because she was what she was, she agreed with me in my doubts. "Simply," she said, "Labadiste knew what he wanted in a wife."

In her surmise, Labadiste saw in Jeanne the grace and dignity to match his station in life. There was little of the peasant in her, and he had talked to her enough times to know that her intelligence matched his.

Having been raised in a family with proper manners, Labadiste bided his time until Jeanne was of marriageable age. When she became sixteen, Labadiste made his intentions known to her parents. He was in turn properly received in the only formal room in the house, a frigid parlor with a round table covered for the occasion with a lace tablecloth, a buffet of dark wood, and walls bearing framed photographs of ancestors with unsmiling faces.

The parlor had changed but little with the passage of nearly a century. Sometimes, I would go into the room alone and shut the door to think about those portraits, imagine what had happened here, and try to put it all into perspective. These were not pleasant experiences, the solitary visits to the parlor. Garat of the carved granite face and his wife with her timid rabbit eyes had joined their ancestors by then. And so had their daughter, my grandmother Jeanne, and her brother Jean-Baptiste. My mother, Maitia, had not. I told myself that was because she was still living and in America then. But it was not the real reason, and in my heart I knew it.

When Labadiste came to present his suit, he was served the proper Spanish sherry and cookies reserved for such occasions as funerals and suits for marriage. There was little quibbling about arrangements. Labadiste was by far the best prospect her parents could hope for. And his proposal did not come as that much of a surprise. Labadiste's calculated encounters with Jeanne on market days and after Sunday Mass had not gone unobserved.

No one bothered to ask Jeanne if she reciprocated Labadiste's affections. That is the American way, as I was contemptuously reminded more than once. In the Basque way of doing things, love was far down the ladder of importance.

Jeanne was told of her engagement one spring evening after dinner in the warm kitchen that was the living core of the house in all seasons, but particularly in the cold months of winter and spring. She was sitting in the same straight-backed wooden bench where generations of unquestioning young women of her family had sat.

She accepted the news of her engagement with an inscrutable expression. Distracted by her own internal seething at not being asked how she felt about the arrangement, she did not see the gleam of avarice in the eyes of her younger brother, Jean-Baptiste. With Jeanne gone, he could claim by forfeit her right to the farm and lands.

Knowing full well how headstrong his daughter could be, Garat had sense enough not to deliver the news to her as if it were an ultimatum. He dwelled instead on Labadiste's own words when he came to press his suit. They did not include such peasant values as house and land and crops. "You will have a rich life," Garat said. "Fine clothes. Perhaps even servants. You will see great cities and countries—things that few people from this poor corner of the world could ever hope to see."

The prospect of having to leave her house and home was like the taste of bitter almonds in Jeanne's mouth. I knew that, because at the end of her life, Jeanne wanted to die in her ancestral home surrounded by her ancestral lands. That she had asked of my mother as a last kindness. I had known that story since I was a child.

The arrangement was sealed. The next time Labadiste was in the village, he and Jeanne and her parents perched on the uncomfortable chairs in the frigid parlor. Jeanne's mother prattled through the endless details having to do with the marriage ceremony, the list of wedding guests, and the obligatory wedding feast. When the ordeal was done, Labadiste took his leave with his usual distant manner, shaking hands but not embracing Jeanne's parents, and brushing Jeanne's cheek with the thin, cold lips that were an integral part of his refined, almost skeletal face.

The only detail that remained unresolved was the wedding date, and that would have to be set for a time that was convenient for Jeanne but mostly for Labadiste, whose busy schedule permitted only rare visits to the Basque Country, even for such an event as getting married. This lack of detail in the arrangements wafted through the walls of Garat's home and into the village, which afterwards savored its irony.

Though they would have preferred that the wedding date be set immediately, Jeanne's parents were only too willing to wait until the time was right for Labadiste. As it turned out, they should have insisted.

As I write this, I find that I know next to nothing about my mother's real father. He is like a ghost who makes himself visible only in tantalizing glimpses and then retreats into a gray fog of mystery, leaving so much untold behind him. Now that everyone from that time is dead, I fear he is lost to me forever.

That I know so little about him is not for want of trying. Well, that is not exactly true. There were lines I could not cross with my mother, who was the only one who really knew anything, even though her knowledge was necessarily filled with gaps. The others, in Donibane, had heard one bit of gossip or another but could not remember with certainty. There was a genuine searching of memory, shaking of heads, and refusal to say anything they were not positively sure of.

About Jeanne and the family Garat and my mother, Maitia, they told me nearly everything once they knew that I knew the core of the secret. But as for Arnaud—my mother once let it slip that that was his first name, and I did not dare ask his last—it was as though he had never existed. Perhaps that is Basque, to erase from memory an outsider who intruded into the ordered scheme of things and left wreckage behind, but it is of little help to me.

When I probed deep in my memory for every little scrap my mother had told me, I knew more than they.

Arnaud was an agricultural specialist on assignment from the French government. His task was to instruct farmers in the underdeveloped regions of France in new methods of raising livestock and crops. He was married. He was educated and came from a good family. He was killed in World War I.

As for what Arnaud looked like, I have only one clue. It came from a quiet interlude in my mother's house in America, after I had come back with my father from his trip to his own high mountain province. My mother and I were looking at photos from the Old Country. Now that I knew her story, or at least a good share of it, she could talk more openly about the identity of people in the old photos.

There was one photograph of her half brother Michel standing with other French soldiers in the rubble of a shelled city. It must have been a rest between battles, because everyone was relaxed. A French officer was with the men. It was hard to make him out because he was standing behind Michel, wearing a kepi such as the one De Gaulle and the Free French made famous later in another war, and he had the little moustache that was affected by so many French soldiers then as a tribute to one of their most famous generals.

My mother on a sudden impulse reached for the photo and took it from my hands. She peered at it intently. "Peter, look at me!" she said. Puzzled, I did. With a strange expression, she said, "My God, you have the same eyes *he* has."

I thought she meant her brother Michel, but she didn't. She meant the officer. He was Arnaud. A piece of the puzzle fell into place with something my mother had witnessed in France before she came to America, an incident in which the same photograph had figured. From that, my mother already knew that the French officer was her father.

.   .   .   .

Knowing the Basques as I do now, I can imagine what Arnaud had to confront in trying to persuade the farmers to change their ways. He had ventured to the outlying areas where they clung most tenaciously to the old ways, and being city bred and not used to that much walking, he had rented a one-horse buggy. The farmers of the valley had listened to his theories on crossbreeding of livestock and crop experimentation with polite attention, and then, as soon as he left, had forgotten everything he told them. He had been warned at his school of agriculture in Paris that this would happen, so he was not surprised. Their forgetting was typical peasant stubbornness about changing the way they had always done things and would always continue to do them. The best that Arnaud could hope for was that one tiny seed of what he said might take root merely because it made practical sense.

Even so, I like to think that Arnaud had determined to enjoy himself by satisfying his own natural curiosity about new places and new people. A man like that would have loved this forgotten country of emerald green mountains, splashing rivers, and the deepest forests he had ever known. He must have climbed a few times to the top of a hill and looked down on the village with its scrupulously whitewashed houses and mottled, red tile roofs, watched the nodding, unhurried gait of gaily yoked oxen on the country lanes, the farmers with gentle goads and inevitable black berets walking beside their animals.

Arnaud must have liked the Basques who inhabited this storybook land: the men on market day mingling in front of the stone ramparts of the Citadel, emanating a strength of character that was like a physical force; the men whose barbarian antecedents had prevented the legions of Pompey and Caesar and the Germanic tribes that came after from establishing a foothold here; those ferocious ancestors who did not flinch from throwing themselves on their spears before capture, whose sons crept through enemy lines at night to kill their own fathers to save them the shame of being prisoner; those wild men who simply disappeared into the deep forests and high mountains and then came slipping back to wage a guerilla warfare that would have discouraged the organized troops of any conqueror.

Arnaud would have been both fascinated and overpowered by the Basques' ability to.work. The way they went at it was almost flagellant in nature. They seemed to enjoy punishing themselves with work. It was like a cleansing from which they derived a perverse sort of pleasure.

And yet, they were not outwardly violent. In the several months he had been in the valley, he had never seen a fight of any kind. He had asked the proprietor of the inn where he lived about that seeming contradiction, and the proprietor had answered after the pause of a man not given to reflection, "There are very few things in this life that are worth fighting about, so we ignore them. But if something is worth fighting about, then watch out."

It was also a country of song: a youth singing alone as he tended his cows in the fields; the high tenor of a shepherd boy on a hillside, carrying down the slopes like the sound of a flute; a man walking home

by himself from the village, singing unself-consciously to vent his good
spirits; children's voices light and pure on their way home from school.

.   .   .   .

Arnaud and Jeanne must have met on a Monday market day. There
was no other place they could have met. At Sunday Mass or at vespers,
the protective Garat and his wife were present to ensure there were no
clandestine meetings of any sort. Even if Arnaud had chanced to come
to Garat's farm on his rounds, he never would have gotten past the big
gates that divided the path to the farmhouse from the country lane.
Garat would have met him there with all the hostility that a father with
a beautiful daughter could have displayed.

The market was the only place where Jeanne could walk without
scrutiny, and Arnaud knew that it was fruitless to visit the farms on
Mondays because their inhabitants would be at market.

And so was he one Monday afternoon, lunching on the terrace and
watching the parade of girls singing and holding hands, with their free
and graceful way of walking and their proud, erect backs: brown-haired
girls, girls with shining black hair, girls with golden hair and flaming
red hair that may have been the legacy of Wellington's soldiers in the
Napoleonic Wars; brown eyes and blue eyes and gray eyes, and always
the radiant skin that had known only soft, clean country air and never
the ground-in soot of city streets or the corruption of the face paint that
so many Parisiènnes had known.

On the village street below the terrace, a girl stopped with bent head
to inspect the bright red sandals at a gypsy's booth. Arnaud watched
with the pleasure of detachment as the tipping sun played at making
reddish lights in her luxuriant auburn hair.

Then, as if Arnaud's gaze had found its way into her consciousness,
she raised her eyes and looked full into his.

.   .   .   .

How Jeanne went about arranging their secret meetings was no small
accomplishment. They were woven through market days when the vil-

lage streets were filled with people and activity, and the deep forests rising from behind the Citadel were only a few steps away. There was no walking hand-in-hand down country lanes. Around every bend there would be a farmer or his wife or children bent on some errand to outlying barns or to the village.

I can well imagine what they had to talk about after the first meetings and the first embraces of young love. They faced so many obstacles that the path in front of them seemed like a nightmare. On Jeanne's part, her marriage to Labadiste had already been arranged. Her father, Garat, would not only have opposed any other arrangement, he could not even be talked to about it.

And if he found out, Garat could be counted upon to go to extremes in his reaction. If Arnaud had ventured to tell him that he and Jeanne were in love and wanted to marry, Garat might well have killed him. His flares of temper, though surfacing rarely, were legend in the region. Garat might have cast Jeanne into the outer darkness, as the saying went, and disinherited her on the spot.

But then, where could Jeanne go? If her difficulties seemed insurmountable, what about Arnaud's? He was a married man with a wife in Paris. Divorce was almost out of the question in a Catholic country, and even if Arnaud and his wife separated and lived apart, he could not keep Jeanne as a mistress. Her sense of honor and her rigid Basque pride would never have allowed that. She could not live as a kept woman— bereft of family, without friends, and most of all without the respect and standing she had always known.

She would be penniless. Arnaud's proper father might have disinherited him, too, after all the trouble he must have taken to ensure that his son married a woman of social standing. And to substitute in her stead a peasant girl ignorant of the manners of Paris life was unthinkable.

As I thought about the courtship of Jeanne and Arnaud, another alternative raised its head. What if Arnaud were acting out the old, old story of a polished city gentleman sweeping a typically innocent peasant girl off her feet, and then leaving her when his conquest was satisfied. That possibility made shudders go up and down my spine.

That Jeanne loved Arnaud was a certainty. From everything I have learned, she may have been headstrong but she was no fool. She had to have known that any arrangement with Arnaud might be only in dreams that could never touch reality.

In the little that my mother spoke of them, the thought of Arnaud not returning Jeanne's love never crossed her mind. My mother could not have dissimulated if she tried. She accepted the fact of their love and their being able to overcome somehow the obstacles that faced them.

Of Arnaud's leaving the village for a trip to Paris during this crucial time, she saw nothing suspicious. Arnaud went because he had to confront his wife and his family and begin the long journey to a legal divorce, even if it meant going clear to the Vatican. All of it would take time.

When finally I learned what happened when that element of time that Jeanne and Arnaud had taken for granted was not to be permitted them, I knew at last that my mother was right.

.   ·   ·   .

Two weeks after Arnaud left for Paris, Jeanne suspected that she was pregnant. After another month, the suspicion became a certainty. She wrote a letter of desperation to Arnaud but never mailed it. When she walked into the little post office, she took one look at the old gossip who was postmistress and promptly walked out again. That sharp-eyed woman would put two and two together and jump unerringly to a conclusion.

After another month had passed, her mother was also certain that Jeanne was pregnant. At first, she consoled herself with the thought that Labadiste was the one responsible. If so, what would it matter if the child came early? What was important was that the marriage would now certainly be assured. It would not be the first time that a child had been conceived in the time of engagement. And finally, the baby would be born in distant Bordeaux, which would give the event an elusive quality of remoteness from the Basque Country.

But when the mother thought about it, she knew with a cold clutching of fear that Labadiste was not the father. He had been back to the village only once since the arrangement was sealed. And he was not the passionate kind of man who would claim the right of premature bedding. When Jeanne's mother came to that conclusion, her control fell apart and she told Garat; and that quiet man, to whom the respect of his neighbors was so important, went a little mad.

Jeanne denied nothing. With her head held high, she told them of her love for Arnaud, the fact that he was married, his plans for divorce, and his coming to Donibane to claim her. At Jeanne's last pronouncement, her father came close to losing the rest of his sanity. "Never! Never!" Garat shouted. "If your Frenchman dares to come to this house, I will kill him."

He very nearly did. A few weeks later, Arnaud returned to the village, not bothering to conceal his mission. Knowing nothing of Jeanne's pregnancy, he dared to drive to the House of Garat. He came as a gentleman to ask for Jeanne's hand in marriage. The divorce proceeding was moving much faster and easier than he could have dreamed, and even his father was beginning to accept the inevitable. He really had no other choice, since Arnaud was his only son. The only condition he had imposed was that Arnaud and Jeanne come to live at his country house until their marriage was old enough to be accepted among his circle of friends in Paris.

Arnaud's father had another reason why the couple should live at the country house. He knew nothing of the Basque Country, but he knew enough of provincial people to be assured that Jeanne and Arnaud could never live in the Basque provinces in tranquility.

Arnaud never reached the house. His carriage was met on the country lane in plain sight of all their neighbors by Garat, armed with a double-barreled shotgun. The fact that it was loaded and that Garat fully intended to use it was beyond question.

"At least let me explain," Arnaud implored. "At least let me see her!"

"If you try to see her ever again," Garat screamed, "I will shoot your brains out."

Jeanne never knew until it was too late that Arnaud had come back for her. She had been confined to her room. A stand of trees divided the house from the country lane. She knew nothing of the exchange. Jeanne spent her time alternately pacing the room, writing letters that would never reach Arnaud, or weeping on her bed.

Her confinement was total. She was not permitted to leave the boundaries of the farm, and even if she had been, there was no place to go. She had no money of her own. And even if she had, she did not have the slightest conception of how one could get as far away as Paris. And once there, what would she find? There had not been a single letter from Arnaud.

Every tradesman in the village knew, however, because the postmistress had told them with no little glee that Garat had made an arrangement with her to intercept Arnaud's letters and destroy them. There was one further condition. The letters were not to be read. That condition, naturally, was broken.

· · · ·

"All right, so she went and got herself knocked up," said Labadiste. "Is that so surprising? She is a very attractive girl. It's a wonder it hasn't happened before."

Garat listened in disbelief at the urbane dismissal of the tragedy that had fallen upon his family. Staring across the polished dark wood table in Labadiste's immigration office in the village, he did not know whether to be insulted or to follow along in Labadiste's practical way of thinking.

"At least she had good taste," Labadiste went on. "I know that young man's family name. It's an honored name in France." He paused and smiled thinly. "Not known in the Basque provinces, of course."

"What are you trying to say?" Garat demanded.

Labadiste leaned across the table to emphasize his thinking. "Let Jeanne deliver the child," he said. "When that is over with, we will proceed with the marriage. Not before. I have no desire to be known as a man who has been cuckolded. The marriage will not be held in this village, where we will be subjected to the vicious tongues that villages seem to breed so prolifically. The wedding will be in Bordeaux, where nobody will know. Or care, for that matter." He waved his hand in dismissal. "In any case, I am going to Argentina for a few years, to open a foreign office there." He waved his hand again in a gesture that was intended to embrace the village. "That should be far enough away from the Basque Country and its provincial customs; sufficient time will pass to make this affair ancient history."

Since there was absolutely no emotion in Labadiste's words, Garat himself could not pretend to emotion. The fact that his family honor would be in part restored was more than he had ever expected. "But the child," he asked in a flare of intuition. "What is to become of the child?"

"The child will not be coming with us," Labadiste said firmly. "I have nothing against the child, mind you, but that would really be too awkward."

"But who will care for it?" Garat stammered. "The child is my blood after all."

"It will stay with you," said Labadiste. "I will send money for its care, on a regular basis. And your time and effort will be well compensated. Please be assured on that count." He added as if in comforting afterthought, "The child will be better off here with you in all ways, especially during its infancy. When it is old enough, I promise you that I will take it as my own. There will be no discrimination, excepting rights of inheritance. I will not honor that primitive custom."

Labadiste stood up to signal that enough time had been taken out of his busy schedule. "Now, if you will excuse me," he said, "I must take care of my young émigrés. With the life they are going to in the wild Americas, they need reassurance, too."

Garat shuffled out of the office. He would not have noticed that the door had been ajar if it were not for the fact that the young men sitting in the waiting room were staring intently at the floor. Those parents who had accompanied them were not embarrassed, however. Garat's gaze swept them with a blaze of anger, but they did not look away.

5

Maitia was born on a winter's night when the whitewashed stone house that shone so brightly in the day was only a chalky smudge on a canvas of absolute blackness. It was a night when the wind that heralded the storm was a screeching wraith that snuffled and cried in baffled fury around the edges of doors and shutters. It was an old and vindictive wind that to Garat, huddled close to the fireplace in the kitchen, boded no good for his ancient and honorable house.

The great iron-studded portals and the fortress stone of the house had withstood much fiercer storms and even armed attack in times long past and were not dismayed. But then there came an intruder whose entry was not to be denied by stone and iron and oak.

Garat was the first in the household to hear the noises in the night that at once blended and isolated themselves in an unholy way with the wailing of the storm.

For an instant he was puzzled, and he raised his head in order to hear more closely. The medley of sounds was raucous and brazen and hellish beyond reason, and then Garat recognized it for what it was.

He did not have to imagine the soot-blackened faces and the dark-clad figures in the lane beyond the great trees, who were clanging cow-bells and sheep bells, beating with sticks on pots and kettles, blowing horns in nightmarish discordance, unleashing cries that mocked his house and his very soul.

It was *galarrotza,* the village's supreme censure for Jeanne's violation of the moral code. Garat also needed no instruction as to the potency of *galarrotza*. In his youth, he had been one of a band that had shamed an old widow who had dared to marry a young man. The medicine of rough music had taken well. The young man had run away from the village and the widow had hanged herself.

"Not so with me!" Garat cried out. Leaping to his feet, he tore the shotgun away from the chimney pegs that supported it and ran to the front door.

It was the storm that brought him back to his senses. When he flung open the door, the rain was coming down in torrents. He had not taken ten steps when he realized that he was soaked to the skin and that the rough music had ended. He heard the clacking of wooden shoes as the young men of the *galarrotza* scattered homeward in the darkness. One last mocking cry carried to him.

Wearily, Garat went back into the house and sat down again in front of the fireplace. Steam rose from his drenched clothes and the smell of wet wool filled the room. Garat was oblivious to everything. He buried his face in his hands and miserably contemplated the morning, when he would have to undergo the shame of raking away the newly cut grass that was strewn in a straight path from the lane to his door.

Forbidden by her husband even to call for a midwife practiced in such things, Jeanne's mother helped to deliver the child in a cold upstairs bedroom. Despite the omen of the storm, Maitia came easily and swiftly into the world. She was born with her eyes open, and the only cry she uttered was when her grandmother slapped her on the back to start her breathing. When the grandmother had sponged the baby clean, she wrapped her in a soft blanket and sat her upright on her knee.

The child's eyes seemed fixed upon her grandmother's face. The grandmother could have sworn there was understanding in them. But that was impossible, she told herself. The baby was, after all, only a baby.

It was at that moment that the brazen sounds of the *galarrotza* carried dimly into the room. The baby's eyes widened and her brows drew together as if she had heard and understood. The grandmother's hands began to tremble as horror shivered her frame. Quickly, before she dropped the child, the grandmother laid her beside Jeanne. When the child gave a sigh and the sigh was a sound as of old resignation, the grandmother turned her back upon the bed and crossed herself. When she turned back the child was asleep and the grandmother told herself, as she would tell herself a thousand times in the years to come, that what she had seen was the product of her fevered imagination.

· · · ·

Jeanne contemplated her child with exhaustion and little maternal feeling. The circumstances had not permitted that. She had been told in no uncertain terms exactly what had happened and what was to happen. She had been abandoned by her lover, she was to bear their child, she was to leave that child as soon as it was weaned, she was to leave the village forever, she was to marry Labadiste and go to a country she knew nothing about, she was to forget that the child of her union with Arnaud even existed.

Jeanne turned her head away so that her tears would not mark the child with unerasable sadness. "Arnaud. My Arnaud," she cried. "What a wreckage our love has left behind."

Her muffled cry was caught up and swallowed by the vindictive wind.

She must have been forewarned by Little Marie or even by my mother, who knew me better in many ways than I knew myself. Or perhaps Sister Xavier was clairvoyant enough to know that I had come to the convent for more reasons than to bear greetings from my mother.

Sister Xavier had met me at the arched gateway of whitewashed stone with a simple oaken cross rearing upright from the top of the arch. I had stepped through the iron grillwork and into her instant embrace. She embraced me so lightly that I had the barest sensation of her cheek against mine. Then she took a step backwards and surveyed me. "You have much of my Maitia in you," she said with a bemused smile at my nervousness about opening the subject of my mother's childhood.

"On the outside," I said. "On the inside, I'm not sure." That realization had come to me at that instant. Something in the nun's presence had pushed it into the sunlight.

Afterwards, we sat at a table with a snowy white tablecloth in a corner of the receiving room. Peace reigned here in this setting of whitewashed walls and red-tiled floors and great windows that looked out upon a cloister filled with roses and hortensia and a multitude of flowers I could not name.

Sister Xavier spoke quietly and without emotion. Indeed, emotion had no place in these convent grounds, pervaded with silence and prayer and meditation.

A novitiate nun with shy, dark eyes served us goat cheese and white wine from the convent's own vineyard. Sister Xavier tasted both sparingly and I had an opportunity to study her. Her face was seamed with an intricate network of almost invisible little lines. Her eyes beneath the white band that crossed her forehead were gentle and wise, and if her hair was graying like my mother's, the black and white headdress of her habit concealed it.

Those eyes were penetrating. They probed into mine with neither approval nor disapproval. In the beginning, I had been afraid to bring up my mother's childhood. But when the amenities were past and the moisture of love for my mother had been patted from her eyes, Sister Xavier met me more than halfway. She had been my mother's neighbor and playmate and dearest friend all the years of their growing up. That closeness to each other had almost become permanent, I was to learn.

"Did your mother ever tell you that there was a time in her youth when she almost came here to join me in becoming a nun?"

At first, I was genuinely startled. Then I thought about it for a while. "My mother would have been content here," I said. "From what I've learned I can understand why she wanted refuge. But does your order want those who are running away from life?"

Sister Xavier smiled. "The life of a nun has its attractions," she said chidingly. "A clean and beautiful place in which to live. More than enough work to keep one busy for a lifetime. Few worries and none of the problems that go with having children." She paused and said meaningfully, "Yes, a refuge also for those in torment."

An edge of reprimand came into Sister Xavier's voice. "You must not judge my people too harshly," she said. "When she was a child, the village took your mother to its heart. Her mother's sin was not her sin. The grown-ups even had their affectionate name for her. *Nimignonne.* That is to say, 'pretty little one.'"

Sister Xavier was remembering vividly now. "Your mother was a beautiful child. Serious brown eyes. Golden braids that were already turning to auburn as she grew out of infancy into childhood. And a face that positively transformed into radiance when she smiled."

·   ·   ·   ·

Garat idled along the country lane, taking short steps to match those of the child beside him. His gnarled hand completely enveloped hers, and, as always, he marveled at the softness of infant flesh. Once, he mused to himself, his own hand must have been just as small and just as yielding, but that was so very long ago that it was beyond his imagination to conceive. It seemed to him that he had been born with these bent and calloused fingers that had known only hard work.

The berry bushes had burst into a multicolored bloom that filled the air with their fragrance, and every once in a while Maitia would cease her chatter and breathe deeply of the redolent perfume. At her insistence, Garat did the same, and he tried to recall when he had last consciously smelled the flowers of spring. For him, the rich promise of newly plowed earth had been sufficient.

Quite against Garat's will, the child had crept into his heart and filled the void he had not even known was there. Boy child or girl child, he had been prepared to dislike it from the beginning. He had even managed to put his own daughter, Jeanne, at the outer rim of remembrance. For a man of his nature, forgiveness was out of the question. He had not even deigned to read the letters that came with their foreign stamps and alien address. If anyone had ever accused him of a lacking in his soul, of no compassion, he would not have understood what the accuser was talking about. It would have been like describing the sky to a blind man. Jeanne had betrayed him, and that was that. He had managed very well to put her not only out of his family but out of his mind. With the passage of years, he would have been hard put even to describe what she looked like.

They were nearing the outskirts of the village. A remarkable change came over Garat. The familiar constriction grabbed at his chest and the visage that had softened down the long lane became defensive and hard as stone. This was the face by which the villagers knew and feared him; only a madman would have dared to make even a veiled remark about the shame that had branded his family name.

Actually, he had nothing to fear. The scandal that had surrounded Jeanne and her Frenchman had been chewed on enough to become stale fare in everyone's mouth. Jeanne was long gone, and there were newer morsels of gossip to ruminate upon. But Garat did not possess the imagination to know that.

He braved the gauntlet of the street, nodding curtly only to those who insisted upon greeting Maitia.

The tobacconist whose little shop huddled against the mossy ramparts was not a madman. He was simply an alcoholic whose mind had been burned out by absinthe. After Garat had taken his purchase of pipe tobacco, the tobacconist fixed his swimming eyes upon Maitia, smiled foolishly, and said, "Your daughter? No, of course that couldn't be." His brow became furrowed with the effort of remembering and then cleared with enlightenment. "Oh, I . . ." he began.

Garat cut him short with a stare that was ferocious enough to penetrate through the mist that clouded the tobacconist's mind. "Good day," he said. Taking Maitia's hand, he propelled her out of the dark recesses of the shop and into the daylight.

After that incident, Garat would have preferred to go home as fast as his steps could take him. But the reason for the walk into the village was that he had promised to take Maitia for a confection, and it was not in him to break a promise.

They sat in the gentle spring sunshine on the café terrace beside the waterfall, and Garat watched indulgently as Maitia nursed her dish of ice cream and wafers with serious preoccupation. He dreaded the question that was coming, but he was at least prepared for it.

"Aitatchi," she said, puzzled, using the familiar name for grandfather in Basque. "What did that man mean when he said I wasn't your daughter?"

Garat avoided her eyes. "Don't pay any attention to him," he said gruffly. "He's a drunken fool."

Another question by Maitia was mercifully forestalled by the arrival of the café's owner. Beaming down on Maitia, he asked, "Does the ice cream please you, Nimignonne?"

The serious set of Maitia's face disappeared and she flashed the café's owner an entrancing smile. "It's so good!"

The café owner turned his attention to Garat. "We don't see you in town much, Garat."

"There's enough work to do at home to keep a man busy," Garat said noncommittally.

The café owner nodded. "Yes, that's true. Work, work, work seems to be our destiny." He said goodbye to Maitia and retreated from Garat's dour presence.

"I had never heard my grandmother scream before," my mother had told me. "I thought she had lost her mind. She was trying to tell me that my mother had come home. She was in the village and would be at the farm any moment."

My mother was telling me of the first time she had seen her mother, Jeanne. She had been perched on a bench in the kitchen, engrossed in her primer. Warm light was pouring in through the open window. Her concentration had been so intense that she did not hear the exchange between Amatchi and a boy who had run all the way from the village with the message.

But she did hear her amatchi's frantic footfalls on the stone flagging of the foyer. The kitchen door burst open and her amatchi stood there, her face distraught and her hair disheveled. She grabbed Maitia by the arm and dragged her to the kitchen pump. Maitia's face was scrubbed, her hair unbraided and braided again, and then she was dragged upstairs to her bedroom to change her soiled smock for her best dress.

In her conscious memory, she had never heard mention of a mother. From the beginning, she had assumed that her grandmother was her mother and that her grandfather was her father. For the first time, she realized that that was impossible. Her playmates had grandmothers and they had mothers, and they were distinct and separate people. Maitia had no way of knowing that the fact of her mother's existence was never spoken about in the household. Nobody had ever mentioned her mother before. Nor her father.

When Maitia had asked if her father had come home, too, Amatchi had grabbed her hurtingly by the upper arm and shrilled, "You are never to mention your father!"

It was the first time, too, that Maitia could remember Amatchi laying hands on her in anger. She was stunned. In the space of a few minutes, Maitia's ordered and gentle world had been overturned. Her grandmother was not her mother. Her grandfather was not her father. She was forbidden to speak of her father. And it all had to do with a woman named Jeanne.

Maitia was made to wait in her closed bedroom until she was summoned by her amatchi to the formal little parlor. She heard the clip-clop arrival of the carriage in the yard, the muffled sounds of joy and weeping at the front door, the protestations of a woman's voice wanting to go into the kitchen instead of the formal parlor, and her amatchi's objections, having to do with Jeanne's fine clothes getting soiled in the kitchen.

Maitia had been prepared to be rude, but the voice of the woman called Jeanne dispelled that. Behind its well-bred tones there was a quality about that voice that plumbed far back into Maitia's consciousness.

When finally her amatchi called, Maitia smoothed her skirt and went down the stairs. Holding Amatchi dutifully by the hand, Maitia crossed the foyer and was ushered into the little parlor.

"I imagined for a minute that it was a dream and I was seeing a vision," my mother said, spreading her hands in wonder. "She was standing with the afternoon sun behind her and her hair was like a golden crown. Her dress was made of silk and the sunlight turned it to silver. She was the most beautiful person I had ever seen."

And then Maitia was caught up in a smother of silk and exotic scents. "I am a monster ever to have left you," Jeanne cried.

And then Maitia knew everything was going to be all right. The mystery and the unexplained guilt that had descended upon her so suddenly that day were becoming unraveled. She even knew what to expect when the clumping of wooden shoes upon the flagstone of the foyer cast a spell of apprehension over the room.

Garat must have heard Jeanne's raised voice, because his face bore no expression of surprise when he entered the parlor. He stood in the doorway, regarding her as if from a far distance. Words were not needed to convey the hostility that emanated in cold waves from his graven face.

If she was affected by her father's attitude, Jeanne did not reveal it.

Standing straight and aloof, Jeanne met him on his own terms. There was an interminable silence broken only by the ticking of the clock on the mantle of the fireplace. When it seemed the silence itself would shatter from the prolonging, Garat was the first to surrender.

"So you've come back."

Jeanne nodded. "Yes."

"Well . . ." Garat began, and was unable to go on. Mumbling something incoherent about having to wash his hands, he turned slowly and left the room. Watching his retreating form, it seemed to Maitia that his back was bent as if a great load had been settled on his shoulders.

·   ·   ·   ·

In some ways, it would have been better if Jeanne had never come back to the village again, even to claim the child of her womb. In the seven years of her absence, the scandal had died down to embers in the memory of the village, reduced to idle gossip without sting in it. Now, the embers were fanned into flames as though it had happened yesterday.

The village saw neither romance nor tragedy in what she had done. It was still a day when a boy from one Basque village would not dare to fall in love with a girl from another village ten kilometers away. In the rare cases that it happened, he could count on disinheritance and being shunned for the rest of his days, denied even by his family. And in Jeanne's case, she had made the ultimate error of loving a man who was not even Basque. He might as well have been a visitor from another planet.

At first, Maitia imagined she saw no difference in the way she was regarded by those around her. But as Jeanne's visits became more frequent, Maitia became fully aware that something had changed. She did not need to hear words to give credence to her belief. The Basques are not much for words. Theirs is a language of the eyes. They made their knowledge known to her in little things: grown-up conversations stopping when she came within earshot, knowing smirks from the boys she passed on country lanes, the secret exchange of glances between her schoolmates at school, and, worst of all, the unctuous kindness of teachers and tradesmen that made her back stiffen to conceal the shame inside.

The radiant smile on Maitia's lips disappeared forever. Whenever she ventured from the house, her heart constricted and remained constricted until she could find refuge there again. She had never known shame before, but now it was ever-present, suffusing her so that she was forced to gasp for air to fill her lungs. At first, she peered intently into her playmates' eyes to find the damning knowledge there. When she found it, she cast her eyes down as though she were guilty of a mortal sin. As the months wore on, they remained that way. For the first time, she tasted an alien hatred. It did not become her.

Something had happened, too, to her grandfather and grandmother. Aitatchi seemed suddenly to have aged a hundred years. His back was permanently bent now, and the strong set of his face dissolved before Maitia's very eyes. Once she had paused outside her amatchi's locked bedroom door and heard the sounds of quiet weeping inside. As for her uncle, Jean-Baptiste, he seemed unperturbed by the transformation of his family. The little smile that played constantly on his lips was the smile of one who possesses an unclean secret.

It was at the time of her First Communion that the first visible blow fell. By Church custom, First Communion was a serious affair that lasted for three full days. For all the three days, Maitia wore her white Communion dress and veil. There were daily processions from the *quartier* to the village church, solemn Masses in which the priest was clad in his best flowing robes, much singing, and the fumbling ordeal of confession by children who did not know what sins they were supposed to have committed. And then, on the last day, the sacred Act of Communion, the draping of a large wooden crucifix about the throat of each communicant, and the handing over of the scrolls of paper tied with ribbon that pronounced them all children of God.

Maitia unwound her scroll by herself in the confusion outside the church. Her quick eyes picked out her name and the date and the name of the church. Then they fell upon a word in the space that was supposed to designate the names of her parents.

Not even her mother's name was inscribed. There was only one word in the space, and that word was *Illégitime*.

In one flash of illumination, Maitia knew what the word meant. It was seared on her memory forever.

When finally she was alone in her bedroom her first intention was to burn the scroll. Only her fear of destroying a holy thing stayed her. That and her mother's coming into her bedroom. Jeanne stretched out her hand for the scroll. She unrolled it and the blood rushed to her face.

"I think it's time you came with me to Bordeaux," she said.

T·W·O

7

It was the shaggy little sheepdog with a bobbed tail who had given Petya the first warning of danger. As though he knew the need for silence, the dog had sounded his warning with a low growl. If he had barked, the sound would have carried to those men who moved like cats and whose ears were trained to hear anything that did not fit into the natural pattern of things.

At break of day, Petya had climbed to the white rocks that capped the grassy knoll, searching for the lamb that had disappeared the night before. The responsibility for the missing lamb was his, and he felt it keenly, because the *patron* who owned the flock would make him and the old shepherd share the loss. So, while the old shepherd milked the sheep in the stone paddock that rested against the shepherd's hut, Petya had gone to look for the lamb.

Gathering the dog under his cape of rough wool, Petya lay prone among the white rocks on the knoll. It would have been a simple matter to slide backwards out of sight, but curiosity had grasped him and kept him where he was.

He knew that in the mountains, detection lay in movement, so he lay still, not daring to move a muscle. He had even pulled the hood of the cape over his head so that the occasional gusts of dawn breeze would not ruffle his shock of black hair. Lying with his chin resting on one arm, only his hooded head and eyes showed in the crevice between the rocks.

The struggling caravan of men took palpable shape as it emerged out of the rolling gray mist. Although he had never seen them on the move, Petya knew them instantly for smugglers. Without exception, all of them wore the trademark of smugglers who made night passages over the Pyrenees mountains between France and Spain—black berets, black cloaks, and dark blue cotton pants tied down with thongs from knees to sandals, so that there would be no flapping pants to trip them up if they had to flee from frontier guards.

He should have known that the night before had been a night for smugglers. The gruff, taciturn old shepherd had even said so. The evening had been one of blue haze so heavy and tense that it seemed as though the sky would burst from the pressure it contained. And then the storm had broken with a crack of thunder that rolled like artillery among the high peaks. Lightning had ripped the night sky, there had been a rush of wind, and the sky had opened suddenly so that the rain came down in a cloudburst. The slate and oaken chips on the roof of the little hut had rattled with the force of it, and Petya had wriggled deeper into the pile of straw that was his bed, pulling the heavy cape over his head with drowsy contentment.

The smugglers were skirting the edge of the precipice. Except for a wounded man who was being helped along by one of his comrades, they walked in single file. The wounded man had a big stain of dried blood that began from his thigh and covered his leg. He was having a hard time of it, but he uttered no sound of pain as he hobbled along.

The smugglers were empty-handed, and Petya reasoned from that and the presence of the wounded man that they must have been ambushed by the frontier guards, let slip their packs of contraband, and escaped into the night. That was curious, because the legend was that frontier guards were reluctant to stir from their cabins on stormy nights. That they were being pursued was evident by the frequent turning of their heads to look behind them. Something else was evident, too, and it gave Petya the answer he was looking for. One man trailed the caravan at an unlikely distance, ignored by the others. He did not glance backwards, but stared fearfully at the men ahead of him. His posture betrayed his guilt. He had informed on his comrades.

The leader was a hawk-faced man, taller than all the rest, and the cloak could not conceal the deep chest and long, sloping muscles that lay underneath. His long stride was decisive and his movements as quick as those of a high-strung horse.

Without any faltering in that flow of movement, the leader wheeled as if in sudden decision and strode back along the line of men. As he approached the informer, he slowed his pace disarmingly. The informer stopped short and regarded him with apprehension. But he was reassured by the casual approach of the leader and the smile on his face. When they came together, the leader began talking in a friendly, conversational tone.

The leader looked back only once, and that was to make sure the file of men had been swallowed up by the mist. Then, the leader stretched out his arm and pointed back along the way they had come, as if giving instructions. The informer was eager to please. He turned completely around to look in the direction the leader was pointing. It was his final error in judgment. The leader took one backward step and his foot lashed out with the suddenness of a striking snake. The blow caught the informer in the small of his back and propelled him over the precipice. There was a long, wailing scream that diminished in volume and then ended abruptly.

Petya slipped backwards down the slope, but not before a low moan escaped him. Afterwards, he was never quite sure whether it was the moan or the sound of the vulture that alerted the leader of the smugglers. As he made his descent he saw the vulture hopping out of a hollow of ground in an attempt to get airborne. He was brown all over except for his black head, and his wings were spread to a width of six feet. His curved beak was dripping with red blood, which answered the puzzle of the missing lamb. The vulture had heard the falling man's scream, unerringly interpreted it for the sound of death, and was not wasting an instant to take advantage. While he was on the ground, his movements were unwieldy and awkward. But when he finally lumbered into the air, he was transformed into a thing of grace and beauty.

When Petya reached the bottom of the slope, he found he could barely stand. His legs were like water beneath him. And that was how the smuggler found him. The smuggler was outlined on the ridge above, his black cloak flapping in the breeze and a long, gleaming knife gripped in his hand. Their gazes met and locked, the coal black eyes of the smuggler boring into the gray eyes of the youth as if trying to wrench out of them just how much Petya had seen.

It was the little sheepdog who saved Petya. Squirming free from the arms that held him, the dog darted up the slope and flung himself at the smuggler. It was enough of a diversion to break the locking of the eyes. His brow furrowing in irritation, the smuggler glanced down at the dog and kicked him away as easily as if he had been a puppy. The dog's body lofted into the air and came down to earth with a sickening thump. At the sound of his pain, Petya forgot the smuggler, ran to the dog, and gathered him up in his arms. When Petya dared to raise his eyes again, the smuggler was not even looking at him. His eyes were fixed on the shepherd's hut below. A plume of blue smoke was rising from the shutter in the roof, fusing into the gray mist that still clung in patches in the hollows of the mountains.

Petya needed no instruction on what was going on in the smuggler's mind. He knew with crystal clarity that the smuggler had no way of knowing who was watching from the shepherd's hut below and could bear witness against him. The smuggler stood for a moment in an indecision of terrible intensity. He stared at Petya as if to fix his face forever in his memory. Then he wheeled and strode out of sight over the ridge.

Despite the burden of the dog, Petya sped down the slope with the agility of a young goat, his bare feet touching grass and ruts and rocks with the lightness of a feather.

The shepherd's hut lay in the lee of a low hill. Its thick walls of little stones and big stones chinked with clay had stood for a long time. The old shepherd, who had had some education, once told Petya that the community of huts in this high place had been built by Basque warriors who dressed in skins of wild animals and carried spears a thousand years before. They had fled to the land above the timberline and preyed upon the invading armies that moved between France and Spain by way of the valley floors and easy passes.

Petya did not know whether the old shepherd's claim was true, but he did know that the huts were like miniature fortresses. The windows were narrow slits and the doorways so low that one had to bend double to pass through them.

The old shepherd had just finished milking the sheep when Petya returned. He would begin at one end of the paddock and milk his way to the other end, and then milk his way back to the beginning again, because some of the ewes were reluctant to let go of their milk the first time through. The old shepherd would often get more milk on the second pass than on the first one.

There was a big fire burning on a hearth against one wall, and the hut was uncommonly warm when Petya ducked in through the low door. Despite the flames, it took Petya a moment to accustom himself to the gloom. The old shepherd did not even look up when Petya came in. He was occupied with pouring milk into the copper kettle resting on the fire irons. The kettle contained a sheep's stomach that had been chopped into little pieces to release the rennet that would transform the liquid into the first stage of cheese.

"Did you find the lamb?" the old shepherd asked gruffly.

"A vulture took him," said Petya.

The old shepherd swore to himself. "I don't know how the *patron* can blame us for that. But if I know him, he'll find a way."

The old shepherd turned his attention to the round wooden mold that held the milk already coagulated by the rennet. Rolling up his sleeves, he pressed down with both hands on the soft mass. Skim milk oozed out of the mold and into the slanted groove on the planking below. At the end of the groove was a copper pitcher to catch the skim. The old shepherd replaced it with an earthen crock.

"You better have your breakfast. We're late today. The sheep want to go."

The old shepherd turned to Petya with the pitcher of skim milk. He stopped when he saw the sheepdog in Petya's arms. "What's the matter with him?"

"He got kicked."

The old shepherd was not a man for unnecessary words. He looked at Petya quizzically, but did not pursue the question. He was a tall, spare man with blue eyes and a beak of a nose crisscrossed with tiny veins. He gestured with his head, and Petya knelt to put the dog gently on the packed earth floor of the hut. The old shepherd examined the dog's mouth and nose and ears, then moved his hands skillfully over the dog's body, probing at ribs and pulling gently at legs. The dog raised his head and regarded the old shepherd without protest. In the firelight, his eyes glinted through the shaggy fringe that covered them.

"He's all right," the old shepherd said. "Nothing broken to tear him up in his guts. But he better rest for a while. You will have to take the sheep out alone."

Petya carried the little sheepdog to a corner of the hut and covered him with burlap to control the shock from which he was suffering. When he finished, the old shepherd was frying corn cakes in a skillet. That and the skim milk made up their breakfast.

"Do you want to tell me?" the old shepherd asked when they were done eating.

Petya told him, leaving out nothing.

The old shepherd took out his long clay pipe and stuffed a pinch of tobacco into the bowl. He lighted the pipe with an ember from the fire.

"Did he memorize your face?" the old shepherd asked.

Petya nodded. "Oh, yes."

"Then you are dead."

The blood drained from Petya's face, and his eyes asked a question.

"Because when he has had time to think about it, he will know that he can never live safely if you are alive."

"But I don't know him and he doesn't know me. I've never seen him before."

"That means nothing. A clever man like him will find out who you are and where you are."

"I'll swear to him never to reveal my secret."

The old shepherd wagged his head wearily. "That is no insurance at all. Do you realize what you are holding over his head? You've seen him murder a man. He cannot sleep easily with that knowledge."

Petya's head sank hopelessly between his shoulders. "What am I to do?"

The old shepherd put out his pipe. "I want to think on it." He bent over to peer out the doorway. "It's time the sheep went out. The other shepherds will have a good laugh this morning. We've never been so late."

The old shepherd was right about that. The great sweeps of green mountains above the timberline were covered with white flocks that had appeared by magic from the paddocks lying concealed in the mountains' folds. Each flock was as isolated as if separated by an invisible fence. Though the mountains above the timberline were communal summer pasture, each shepherd had his own grazing domain. "No trespass" was the iron rule, and any shepherd who violated it would be driven from the mountain by neighbors so implacable in their demand for privacy that they could barely bring themselves to speak to one another.

Because of his late start, it was well after noon when Petya's flock stopped for the midday rest. He was high on the mountain, just under the brutal rim that marked the boundary with Spain, and beneath him dropped the expanse of grassy slopes and white rocks that marked the shepherds' summer range. Far, far below was the line where the deep forests began, as clearly defined as if it had been cut by a razor.

For the first time in his life, nothing of the lofty panorama crept into Petya's consciousness. His mind was in torment because he could figure no way out of his dilemma. He could not hide himself forever, and one day, or more probably one night, the hawk-faced smuggler with the gleaming knife would appear out of nowhere to take his life. And though Petya was tall and long-muscled, he was still only sixteen years old and no match at all for a powerful man who had it in him to kill so easily.

Just beneath the meadow where his flock was bedded down, there was a spring bubbling out from under a boulder. Its water flowed down a shallow ravine, exposing the pebbles and clear sand that lay close to the surface in these high mountains. A pool had formed not far down the ravine. Restless and unable to doze at the midday rest like the other shepherds, Petya bounded down to the pool. It was filled with elusive gray trout. Rolling up his pantlegs, Petya waded slowly into the pool. The water was so cold that it numbed his feet, but the sensation was a welcome one. As the old shepherd had taught him, he stopped still and bent over and put his hand into the water. Despite the pain, he kept his hand immobile. A curious trout swam close to his dangling fingers, flitted away, and came back again. With the most insignificant of movements, Petya moved his hand under the trout and lightly stroked its belly.

The trout moved away again, and then, pleased with the caress, came back for more. Petya stroked forward until his fingers were under the trout's head. With a quick thrust, he hooked his thumb and forefinger into the trout's gills and flipped him onto the bank with scarcely a ripple. At the end of an hour, he had caught ten trout of respectable size. That would make for a dinner that the *patron* could claim no part of. And it would assuage the old shepherd's suppressed impatience over the curiosity that had turned Petya's life around in one day.

· · · ·

The shepherd's hut had never seemed so much like a home as it did that night. It was almost like a premonition of loss. In the flickering firelight, Petya's eyes seemed to hold onto everything within, the hollows in the stone walls that held the growing stacks of round cheeses, the hanging, whittled-down ham that provided their occasional respite from corn cakes, the bed frame of stout wooden poles filled with bracken for the old shepherd's bed, the fire smoldering red on the hearth.

They had eaten well. Trout cooked in ham fat, a speck of precious greens from the struggling little garden outside, corn cakes dipped into the mingled juices of trout and ham, and, of all things, coffee with sugar and whole sheep's milk. On the fingers of one hand, Petya could count the times in his life he had tasted that precious brew. The old shepherd had even been tempted to cut into one of the cheeses, but that would have incurred the wrath of the *patron,* who could calculate at a glance how many rounds of cheeses were coming to him.

The old shepherd had been in a surprisingly good mood, too, though he had said nothing through the preparation and eating of the meal. Now, he sat hunched on his hand-hewn wooden stool beside the fire, stretched his bare feet to the warmth, and savored his pipe. Finally, he cleared his throat and spoke, and what he said shattered Petya's reverie like the blast of a gun.

"You must run away."

When he had recovered his wits, Petya said despairingly, "I don't know anywhere else."

"Very far away," the old shepherd said as if he had not heard Petya. "Where he can never find you."

Petya looked down at his bare feet and the tattered shreds of clothing. "I don't have any money and I don't have any clothes."

"America," the old shepherd said. "I remembered today that I met a man once who had gone to America, but I can't remember which America. North, I think. Because they kill each other too much in South America."

Some recollection out of his brief schooling in the village came back to Petya. "But America is across the ocean." He added superfluously, "And I've never even been to the ocean."

"You have two strong legs to get you there."

"And then what?" said Petya. "Do I swim the rest of the way?"

The old shepherd looked at him sternly to determine whether the youth was being sarcastic.

He decided that Petya was only desperate.

"I remember now the name of a man who is said to traffic in boys like you. He will not make you swim there. He will put you on a boat."

"But that must cost money," Petya said. "I have no money." His pride would not permit him to say that his father had no money either.

The old shepherd waved his hand in dismissal. "The way of it," he said, "is that this man, this trafficker whose name is Labadiste, I believe, will pay for your passage to America. He will make all the arrangements for you to find work there with the sheep." At Petya's unspoken question, he said, "You must then send the money for your passage back to him. I don't know how this is done, but Labadiste will know. You can count on that."

Petya surrendered. The old shepherd was right. There was absolutely no hope for him here. A great wall of fear rose before Petya. It was all so complicated, and the prospect of leaving home and going into the unknown had unmanned him. He bowed his head in silence, listening to the dying rustle of embers in the fire pit. He sighed a great sigh and said, "All right. Where do I go?"

"To a village called Donibane," the old shepherd said. "It lies in the next province, over the mountain between our valley and theirs." He added reassuringly, "They are Basques there, also. Or so they claim. They must be poor, because many of them go to America. That is why Labadiste has an office there. He can do very little business here, because who in his right senses would leave these mountains? Unless he were in trouble. Like you."

Petya was suddenly tired to death. He wanted the warmth and protection of his straw bed. He got unsteadily to his feet. "Can we talk about it tomorrow? I want to sleep."

The old shepherd shook his head violently. "You go tonight!"

"Why?"

"Because I feel in my heart the smuggler will be waiting up here for you sooner than you think."

8

Petya crouched in the bracken at the forest's edge and waited for the sunrise. The eastern sky was streaked with sooty gray clouds, and he was caught up in that moment of hopelessness that precedes the sunrise.

His woolen cape was spread around his shoulders and hunkered knees like a small tent, and in its warmth he drooped with fatigue. He had traveled all the night with only one stop to chew on corn cakes and drink from an icy stream.

The descent from the shepherd's hut to the timberline had been done quickly. As soon as the moon had risen, Petya had laid his walking staff on the grassy hillside and clasped it between his toes. Balancing himself with arms outspread, he had slid down the mountainside, the staff hissing through the vast expanses of grass. He had waited for the moon just so he could avoid the occasional rocks that shone white in its light.

The forest had been another matter. No one in his right mind ever penetrated the forest at night. Not only because of the *basa jaun,* the hairy god whose domain was the darkness of gnarled oaks covered with the lichen of centuries, but the more palpable menace of great wolves. Closing his ears to unexplained sounds, Petya had gone through the forest at a dogtrot. Twice he had stumbled on hidden roots and gone sprawling, and once he had fallen from sheer fatigue, to lie panting on the ground for a moment before forcing himself to his feet and back into the mile-consuming trot.

Now, day was breaking and he was within sight of home. All that held him from going down was caution. He had to make sure that things were as they should be in the ordered life of his homestead and that there would be no unpleasant surprises waiting for him.

The house was set back a safe distance from his village, resting in a perfect saddle between two low hills. It was a house of gray stone with a sharply sloping roof of slate, and it was divided into two connecting parts—one for the humans and one for the animals. The body heat from cows and pigs went a long way in keeping the human habitation warm in the cold winters.

As he watched, the bent and black-garbed figure of an old woman, his grandmother, made its slow way up from the creek below to the house. That was a good sign. Once a week his grandmother would go down to the creek and spend the night washing the family's clothes and bedsheets and towels in the icy waters. At daybreak, she would climb back to the house and hang the washing on the clotheslines that faced the sun, and then start her day's work. There was not much she could offer to the welfare of the household now except the washing and working in the garden and sweeping the worn oaken floors.

The sun tipped the eastern mountain rim, and the hopelessness of the night disappeared. The streaks of gray clouds were suddenly transformed into rose in the blue porcelain sky of a new day. A single ray touched the spire of the village church, moved on to a high rooftop, and then to the forest edge where Petya crouched. There was a torrent of birdsong. The heavy wooden shutters that shut out the night damps flew open in the house to let in the sweet air of day. He saw his father come out onto the front stoop that faced the sun, stretch and yawn, and go back inside for his indispensable morning coffee.

All was well in his household. Petya got up from his hiding place and made his way down the hillside.

·　·　·　·

His mother and his grandmother had worked all day on the last dinner Petya was to know at home. It had begun with a paté of the house, salami with butter curled upon it, and soup thick with vegetables. There had been chicken boiled in a spiced tomato sauce, and milk-fed lamb as the main course. Afterwards, there was cheese, and the rare treat of wine.

They had eaten the farewell dinner in the tiny kitchen with the open-sided fireplace, the cooking utensils hanging in its depths. Daylight was fading.

Petya was seated in the place of honor at the head of the table. He

wore the mismatched suit of striped wool that was his father's and had
been his grandfather's. It was the only suit in the house, and was there
only because his grandfather had been buried in his nightshirt. The suit
would have been wasted beneath the ground in the churchyard. It hung
on Petya in folds. His grandfather had been a big and powerful man.

Petya's father said little as he ate. For the first time in his life, he was
confronted with a situation that could not be met with directness and
brute strength. When Petya had first told him that he must run away
to America, his father's giant frame had filled almost to bursting with
outrage. His strength was such that he had broken an oaken goad in his
hands as though it were a matchstick.

He had wanted to go to the village of the smuggler, find him, and
crush him with his bare hands. With reflection, he had come to realize
that this was an impossibility, simply because he did not know which
village the smuggler came from or exactly what he looked like. Even
then, it would have been difficult to kill the man. Each village protected
its own as if all its inhabitants made up a tribe of blood kin, which in
fact they did if one were to look back far enough.

The people of one village had no truck with the men and women
of another village, but treated them as aliens not to be trusted or confided in. Any inquiry that Petya's father made would have been met
by a united front of men who could kill an intruder without a second
thought.

His father had finally abandoned that notion and come up with
another, equally impractical. He would stay at Petya's side until the
trouble between him and the smuggler was settled. Petya had talked
long and earnestly and was finally successful in convincing his father
that this, too, was an impossibility. If Petya stayed in the village, there
would come a night on some black road when the smuggler would find
him and kill him. If Petya went back to the mountains, his father could
not follow. Since there was no one else to share the burden, the father's
duty was here with his farm and animals and his household. At last, he
came to the realization that Petya must find his own way in the world.

Still, his father was not altogether reconciled. The flare that had filled his eyes with murder had only subsided into a smoldering ember. He kept his own counsel. Somewhere, sometime, he would find this man who would have murdered his son. And then the revenge would be sweet and terrible.

The household was one of restraint in all things. This was a rule of behavior so old that it was not even discussed. There had been no tears, not even from his little sisters, and certainly not from his brothers. His mother and his grandmother agreed that to run away to America was the only course open to Petya. The possibility of going to the gendarme of the village had never even been broached, because that would have made Petya an informer, which could not be. Besides, the law was not to be trusted.

His grandmother, who knew more certainly than the others that she would never see Petya again, had consented to join them at table, which was unheard of. She sat in silence and watched Petya's face throughout the dinner. She was permanently bent now, and little and shrunken down. Her gray hair was pulled back, sharply outlining the widow's peak that was a trait of the family. Her forehead was deeply furrowed, her face seamed and her eyes sunk in deep, dark pockets under jutting eyebrows. The outline of her jaw was strong, another trait that ran through the family.

She spoke only once, and that was at the end of the meal. Her voice was as deep as a man's. Taking a small leather pouch with drawstrings from under the folds of her widow's weeds, she laid it down in front of Petya. There was a clinking of gold coins when she did so.

"This was to pay for my funeral," she said cavernously. "But you need it more than I do to get to wherever this place is you are going." She was silent, and then she said, "If you make money, you must return it to me somehow, because I do not want to be buried like a pauper. I want to be buried in a dress."

Meeting the old, old eyes, Petya nodded.

Petya's father muttered something unintelligible and shuffled his feet. He was a broad man with shoulders three feet across and a chest that leaped from his collarbone. "It's time," he said. He went to the fireplace and took down the enormously long gun that family tradition said a forebear had carried all the way to Russia and back with Napoleon. But the forebear, with no schooling at all, had never known exactly where he had gone with the Grand Army. Ignorant of political boundaries, he had said only that he had gone for a long walk to a country where it had gotten a little cold.

Hefting the gun easily in his great hands, Petya's father said, "I will accompany you as far as the line with that province down there. You'll be safe from then on, and anyway I don't want anything to do with those people who claim they are Basque."

There were no goodbyes except for a brushing of cheeks with his mother and grandmother, his sisters and brothers. In a matter of minutes, Petya and his father were swallowed up by the darkness, threading their way along the path that skirted the village.

Petya looked back once, but all he could see of his homestead was a narrow slit of light from the kitchen window. A lump came into his throat, but he managed to gulp down the sob that was coming. The noise of their passage thankfully kept even that from his father's ears.

In my mother's time there, Labadiste's Hotel Amerika was located in a desirable quarter of the seaport town of Bordeaux. It was only a ten-minute walk from the railway station, that immense stone edifice that was one of the keys to Bordeaux's prosperity as a center of commerce. The other was, of course, the port where freighters had come and gone since the days of sailing ships.

The Rue de la Marne had been an excellent address in my mother's time. But with the coming of the automobile and the airplane, it had suffered. When I went to visit my aunts, who still ran the little hotel, the railway station that once shone like a palace was a dreary place. It was smudged with a hundred years' worth of soot from belching smokestacks. The street was no longer as my mother had described it: sparkling clean, with hotels, restaurants, and even a few fashionable shops. When I talked to her later, I could not bring myself to tell her that it had become a prostitutes' haunt.

Then and now, the Hotel Amerika was three stories high, with balconies encircled by ornamented iron railings that looked down upon the street. Wide front doors opened onto a café where guests of the hotel could sit at coffee or aperitifs. Overlooking the café was a raised area with a long table of polished wood. Once, the more important guests of the hotel dined here, but now it was reserved for families. Beyond that was a bustling kitchen where the clashing of pots and pans could be heard from dawn to midnight.

A foyer with a registration desk fronted on the street. From there, a narrow, winding staircase led up to the first story of guest bedrooms, which were ample in size and well appointed. From this first story the staircase led up to a perfect rabbit warren of tiny rooms, where young Basques on their way to the Americas stayed until their travel papers were ready.

It is ironic that it was in this hotel that my mother met for the first time the two men who would have the most to do with her life.

One was Labadiste, who was rich and worldly-wise. The other was my father.

Labadiste's office was apart from the commercial activity of the hotel. It was a room paneled with wood and hung with paintings of exotic places. The paintings still hung in that room when I saw the hotel. For me they betrayed Labadiste's character and his presumption to a status he was not born to. He must have thought them done by budding masters. Actually, they were embarrassing imitations of indifferent art.

There was a large desk of polished wood, where Labadiste presided in an ornate chair that not so subtly simulated a throne. That revealed either his character or his cleverness. In front of the desk sat three straight chairs, all in a row. They were unadorned. It was here that the young Basques would sit awkwardly in the presence of the king, receiving their itineraries and promises of adventure and fortune. They must have been intimidated after the rude furniture they had been brought up with.

It was to Labadiste's office that Maitia was summoned before she had even unpacked her suitcase. Her mother left her alone at the door in a manner that showed that she too was intimidated by the man who was her husband. Maitia would have retreated then and there except that the paneled door to the office suddenly burst open and a furious small figure emerged, banging the door behind him. It was Maitia's half brother, Michel, born to Jeanne during the years Labadiste was operating out of Buenos Aires in Argentina. The boy was slender and had his mother's gray eyes and auburn hair. That he also possessed her rebellious streak was evident in the storm cloud that distorted his features.

"I won't!" he exploded. "He can't make me!"

Michel's outburst was cut short, and he stopped in astonishment as his eyes took in Maitia. His brow cleared and the cloud vanished. A small smile lighted his face like a passing ray of sunlight. He said in slow wonder, "You must be my sister! You must be Maitia!" He paused, and then with a sudden impulse he embraced Maitia tightly and was gone.

Michel did not know it, but that display helped to shape Maitia's apprehension about confronting the man who seemed to dominate everyone.

. . . .

Maitia saw a face with a thin, hard mouth, pale brown eyes, and fine hair that was already thinning. Labadiste was wearing a black suit of expensive wool that fit his frame like a glove. He regarded her for what seemed an eternity, with distant, critical eyes. Without a word of greeting, he motioned Maitia to one of the straight chairs in front of his desk.

Knowing my mother, I could imagine that after being bruised and shamed by the affair of First Communion in Donibane, she was determined not to back down again, even to a man like Labadiste.

But as my mother told me later, things took an unexpected turn. Labadiste nodded. The thin lips broke into something that resembled a smile. She had no way of knowing that the smile was one of rare approval.

"Well, at least your father's breeding shows through. It has not been buried by the peasant in you." Without a break in his speech, Labadiste said, "I will tell your mother to buy suitable clothes for your life in the city. You are not a country girl anymore."

Labadiste spoke in a voice that had been cultivated to match his station, and he spoke not in Basque, but in French. Maitia was to learn that speaking Basque was forbidden within the family. Only in those situations where one of his young Basque men could not speak French would Labadiste condescend to use his native tongue, and then he employed a form of Basque that was overlaid with French accents and phrases.

Before Maitia could bridle at Labadiste's disdain for her village dress, he disarmed her. "Your mother has explained to me how things are with you in the Basque Country," he said. "Pay no attention to it. They are but simple village folk with no concept of the world outside. You will forget them quickly."

But there was not one word of welcome and certainly no acknowledgment that there was any relationship between them. From that moment, Maitia knew that she dared not ever call him Father. Her presence in the hotel, as far as Labadiste was concerned, was only that of a tolerated refugee, and nothing more.

When Maitia had been dismissed, her mother took her to the intimate family parlor to meet her other children. The difference between the two meetings was like night and day. Because they had been raised almost exclusively by their mother, they exuded warmth and embraced Maitia as a sister.

There was Madeleine, who was fair and looked like her father, Labadiste; but what was skeletal in his face became fragility in hers. There was Marie-Claire, who was plump, but had her father's superior bearing. And then there was Michel, who was hot tempered and given to nerves. His passion for rugby and soccer was the only medicine that calmed him.

· · · ·

Michel was long dead when I went to visit my aunts in the Hotel Amerika. They received me in the same intimate parlor where my mother had been received so long ago. But time had not passed at all when it came to their natures.

Madeleine was still delicate and beautiful, and Marie-Claire was still plump and intolerant, though the years had taken the edge off that. I was to visit the hotel often in the year to come.

My aunts knew before I arrived what I was after. On the whole, they were honest and revealing to me. They had loved my mother as children and they loved her memory now. But there was no mistaking one fact. Like everyone else, they had cried in heartbreak and at the same time breathed a huge sigh of relief when my mother went to America.

There had been a special relationship between Maitia and Michel. "It was a secret life between them," Marie-Claire said. "I never understood it. When Michel would come home from boarding school it was always, 'Maitia. Where's Maitia?' The two of them would go off to the park and be gone for hours. What they found to talk about, I never could understand."

For now, though, I wanted to learn about how my mother met my father, if that is what the encounter can be called, in this very hotel.

"Actually, she saw your father for the first time from the balcony to our bedroom," my aunt Madeleine told me. "We were all three playing there when Marie-Claire looked over the railing. "Come look!" she said. "It's some of Papa's slaves."

Marie-Claire glanced at me in a wordless plea for forgiveness, to understand that she was only a child then and knew no better.

The group of half a dozen or more young men from the Basque mountains was coming from the railroad station. They were being led down the sidewalk in the direction of the Hotel Amerika by old Jean, the night watchman, who knew what he was about. When he was young, he too had come from the country to the city.

The young Basques were unmistakable with their ruddy faces and rough hands and their awkward-fitting, mismatched suits in black and blue that had been handed down from generations past. Adhering to the tradition that neckties are not for Basques, they wore none. They carried their few belongings in sacks or battered cardboard suitcases.

"None of them had been more than ten miles away from their villages in their lives," my aunt Madeleine said. "And they showed it. They were scared to death."

My aunt Madeleine told how she began to laugh uncontrollably. "'Look at that one,' I said. 'He walks on the flat sidewalk just as if he were climbing a mountain.'"

"It was true," said my aunt Marie-Claire. "One of them, the tallest one, was throwing his legs out in front of him as if he were walking uphill." She paused. "It was your father."

Hearing the laughter, one of the young Basques had looked up and seen the girls. Instead of being offended, he had wagged a finger at them and called out something they could not hear.

"Then I said a cruel thing," my aunt Marie-Claire sighed, "but you

must understand that I had never been up into the Basque Country then."

Marie-Claire had thrown her chin up into the air and said sternly,
"We're not supposed to talk to them, you hear?"

"Why not?" my mother had asked.

"Because they come from poor peasants," Marie-Claire had pronounced. "Papa says they are lower class, so pretend you don't see them."

My mother completely lost her temper then. She screamed at Marie-
Claire that the Basque boys below were exactly like the boys she had
gone to school with in the village, that they were in no way inferior
to city people, and that they should be felt sorry for instead of being
looked down upon, because they were going to unknown lands and
might never come home. She had stamped her foot and fled from her
sisters.

· · · · ·

Maitia was to see the young Basques again before they left. Because she
was shy of passing through the front doors and past the hotel guests in
the café, the next day she entered the hotel, as often before, through the
back door, into the kitchen.

For their meals, the young men had been relegated to a table in one
corner of the noisy room. Painfully ill at ease, they sat bolt upright,
handling their knives and forks as if they were alien instruments. Un-
certainty and apprehension about what the future held for them in a
strange land across the sea haunted their features. They reminded Maitia
of frightened lambs on market day, knowing nothing of their fate.

Her eyes swept the table quickly as if she had already classified them
as having one face. Then one set of eyes raised themselves. They were
gray eyes set deeply in a lean, long face. A shock of black hair looked
as if it had made up its mind to be permanently unruly. Recognizing
the young man she and her sisters had been laughing at because of his
mountain stride, Maitia's face flushed. But there was no rebuke in his
expression.

Their eyes met for an instant, and then she lowered her chin and walked past the table. *This young man is different from the rest,* she knew then. *He may be diminished by this passage, but there is no servility in his eyes. Nobody will make a slave out of him.*

1 0

Petya woke in the first gray light of dawn and knew instantly that it had turned bitter cold in the night. The inside of the conical canvas tent was like a tomb, and the tentacles of icy cold had even penetrated through his bedroll of heavy canvas and woolen blankets. He listened for the sounds of sheep. From the slow, deep-pitched ringing of the bells on the leaders and an occasional bleating, he knew they had barely begun to stir.

Petya decided to let them go their way until he had had his coffee. After all, there was no chance of his losing them in the snow-covered desert that stretched for a hundred miles in every direction. And if the snow was frozen, their progress would be slow as they pawed their way down to the dried ends of sagebrush that was their main forage in the winter desert.

Without getting out of bed, he reached over to the square box of thin iron sheeting that served him for warmth and a place to cook in this time of storms. He flipped open the round plate at the end of the stove, stuffed in a few gnarled twigs of sagebrush, and set a match to them. The sagebrush was impregnated with its own oil, and in an instant it burst into flame. Petya waited until the twigs flamed, put in sturdier stumps of sagebrush, and closed the hole. The stove creaked in protest as its cold iron sides expanded with heat. In no time at all, the tent was warm inside, the water in the blackened coffeepot was singing, and Petya got out of bed.

The night before, he had put his Levi's and stockings under the blanket beneath him so that they would dry out from the heat of his body. He pulled on his trousers and a workshirt over the long flannel underwear that he wore night and day. Over his woolen stockings, he wrapped long strips of burlap that would breathe and yet keep his feet warm until his frozen boots thawed out.

Despite the fearful blizzards that had raged for the past two days, Petya felt as secure and rich as a king. When he had first reached the wilderness of western America, he had not known what to expect. The first thing the boss, Laborde, had done was to take him to a store in Reno and outfit him with clothes he had never dreamed existed: denim trousers that seemed as tough as iron, workshirts, long cotton underwear for summer and flannel for winter, an American Stetson hat that replaced his Basque beret, and wonder of wonders, sturdy leather boots and a heavy sheepskin winter coat. The boots had raised blisters on feet that had never before known any protection other than sandals and wooden shoes stuffed with soft fern, but in time, the leather had formed to his feet and the blisters had become callouses.

Still, the utter solitude in which he found himself bothered him, and his reaction was that of a lonely boy. His only human contact was the camptenders' visit every two weeks with fresh provisions, and Petya had been plunged into longing for the sound of another human voice. That came only when the camptenders rode in on horseback and then went on to supply the next herder fifty miles distant.

But Petya had grown in other ways. In the three years he had spent in the American deserts and mountains, his gangling body had changed into that of a man. His shoulders had broadened, his chest had deepened, and his long legs and arms had taken on added layers of muscle and a steely resiliency. He had become a good shot with the .30-30 Winchester carbine that was his constant companion in the coyote- and mountain-lion-infested wilderness in which he lived, and he was more than accurate with his Colt .45 pistol when it came to close encounters.

For days at a time, his mind had churned in rage at the memory of the smuggler chieftain who had been his undoing in the green mountains of the Basque Country. Then finally the rage would pass and peace return. Petya had been warned about that kind of obsessive thinking and what it could do to the sanity of a man alone. He had satisfied himself with the knowledge that if he were to meet the smuggler now, things would be different.

When he finished dressing, Petya untied the tent flaps to see how his band of a thousand sheep was faring. The sun was rising over the distant mountains, and its slanting rays, reflecting off the frozen sheen of snow, struck at his eyes like a blow. He ducked his head until his vision cleared and then, squinting, looked again to search out the sheep. Driven by hunger, they had wandered farther than he had anticipated into the undulating expanse of snow-covered desert. He debated whether to send the dog, Campolo, out to turn them back, and then gave up the idea. It was going to be hard enough to bring the sheep to bedground near the tent at the end of the day without exhausting the dog now.

Petya ducked into the tent and threw handfuls of coffee into the pot to boil. Coffee, as much as he wanted, was a luxury he had never gotten used to.

He plunged his hands into the packbags for more luxuries—sugar and canned milk and bacon. The huge loaf of hard-crusted bread had been whittled down to a small chunk over the past two weeks, but it did not bother him. The camptenders were due with their pack train tomorrow, and although his supply of eggs was gone, there was bread and bacon enough to last until then. Both the bread and the slab of bacon had frozen solid during the night, but he managed to cut off enough slices to provide him with the only hot meal he would have until nightfall.

The smell of bacon frying in the pan lifted his spirits, and Petya ate voraciously, washing his food down with steaming cups of sweetened coffee. His strength replenished, he went outside for the battered washbasin. Filling it with some of the burro's barley, he poured bacon grease on top and set the mixture down for Campolo. It vanished in a flash. Sheepdogs were always as hungry as wolves because of the meager fare of a sheepcamp. If it were not for the rabbits and rodents they chased down, they would have starved.

Bundling on his sheepskin coat, Petya slung the carbine over one shoulder. Over the other shoulder he hung a canvas bag that held his lunch of bread and cheese and wine. Picking up his walking staff, he went outside, tied the tent flap closed against the possibility of another sudden snowstorm, and trudged after his sheep.

One glance at the snowcapped western Sierra in the far distance told him he need not have bothered to close his tent. The sun had risen and the sky was a dome of cold and brittle blue. There was not a cloud in sight from horizon to horizon.

Walking directly into the reflected glare of the eastern sun, it took him two hours to reach the sheep and his burro. They had been traveling swiftly in search of feed, with no instinct to tell them that things would get no better no matter how far they went. And they were scattered more than he liked. A lone and isolated bunch of a few sheep separated from the rest made an easy mark for the hungry coyotes that invisibly dogged the presence of meat and hot blood. With a wave of his arm, Petya sent the dog around one flank of the band to bring the sheep closer in. Plunging effortlessly through the deep snow and soaring over the higher sagebrush when he needed to, Campolo circled the wanderers like a dark wraith, sending them stampeding back toward the main band.

Petya had arrived just in time. A change in the dog's measured barking told him that Campolo had run headlong into a coyote. The snarling sounds of a fight carried clearly to Petya's ears. Unslinging his carbine, he unleashed a staccato shout to call back the dog. He saw the coyote break cover and leap away in flight. Petya raised the carbine and drew down on the coyote, waiting until he reached the crest of a low hill so that he would be clearly outlined. It was then that Petya knew something was going wrong with his eyes. The gray outline of the coyote was blurred. Petya blinked his eyes to clear them and fired anyway. In the cold stillness, the shot was like a thunderclap. The coyote loped untouched over the crest and disappeared.

Lowering the carbine, Petya covered his eyes with his hand. The darkness was like a healing balm, but when he took away his hand and opened his eyes, the pain he had ignored flared up again so that his very eye sockets were pits of searing pain.

Turning his back on the sun, Petya considered his situation. He had heard of men going temporarily blind in the snow, then wandering aimlessly until night and fatigue and cold claimed them. Sometimes, their bodies, or what was left after the coyotes got through with them, were not found until the spring thaw melted the snow.

When he opened his eyes again, Campolo had made his return. He sat in the snow at Petya's feet, panting and with his tongue lolling. There was a smear of blood on the side of his face, and Petya kneeled down to inspect him. The wound was not serious. The coyote had managed to score only a single groove when their fangs had clashed. As if for the first time, Petya noticed the long fringe of hair that protected the dog's eyes. That was the secret of why the snow glare never seemed to bother Campolo. Taking off his hat, Petya tried to pull his own hair down over his forehead. He was not successful. His hair was simply not long enough to cover his eyes.

Turning around cautiously, Petya regarded the sheep. They were still trailing swiftly to the east, pausing only to nibble at the few tips of sagebrush that emerged above the snow. There was no turning them back now. He would have to wait until they paused for their brief noonday rest, then try to drive them toward the tent by a circuitous route over land that was new to them. Bending his head for protection from the sun, he resigned himself to following after. A million particles of frosted light stabbed like daggers at his eyes.

·   ·   ·   ·

The sun had begun to set over the western horizon, bathing the landscape with a diffusion of light and blue shadow. Petya saw nothing of the diffusion, but he could feel the oncoming cold enough to know that night was not far away.

By now, the world had become a blur of indistinct shapes through which Petya stumbled blindly, his only reckoning being the sound of bells and the tremulous bleating of the sheep somewhere in front of him. His vision had held only long enough for him to turn the sheep in the general direction of the tent after their noonday rest. His instincts told him he must be nearing the bedground in which his tent rested, but he could not be certain of that. The band could have veered off into new terrain. If they had, he would be dead by morning. He felt panic surge up in him and suppressed it quickly. If he lost his nerve now, it would only ensure disaster.

The sheep came to bedground with the darkness. There was no way Petya could know whether it was their old bedground or a new one of their own choosing. With the coming of night, what little remained of his vision vanished. Petya stood in indecision, vaguely aware that he was surrounded by sheep preparing to lie down. He could hear the whimpering of Campolo at his feet, and the thought came to him that perhaps the dog could lead him to his tent. The prospect of warmth and shelter and of crawling into the cave of his blankets was almost overpowering. Petya's legs ached from cold and constant walking throughout the long day, and he could feel the approaching numbness on his face and in his fingers. Slowly, so as not to frighten the sheep into running away, he made his way with short and careful steps to the outer perimeter of the band. When he was clear of the sheep, he kneeled down and found the dog with his hands. The unexpected warmth of Campolo's body came as a surprise to him, and he buried his fingers in the shaggy coat until feeling came back to them. He inched his hand forward to the dog's collar and grasped it. Campolo squirmed but did not try to run away. Speaking in a voice that croaked with exhaustion, Petya tried to instruct him to lead them back to the tent. The dog's whimpering turned to a puzzled whine. Petya realized that it was hopeless. It was simply impossible to transmit his need to the dog.

Petya let go of the collar, turning him loose, and stood up. There was no alternative but to find the tent on his own. He began to walk in what he hoped was a zigzag pattern. With luck, he might bump headlong into the tent. An hour passed in a fruitless search.

Fighting down the terror that gripped him now, Petya stopped again to think. Somehow, there had to be a way to live until the camptenders reached him tomorrow. The camptenders would come first to the tent, that was certain. If they did not find Petya there, they would search out the sheep. But where the sheep would be by tomorrow was anybody's guess. They could be a dozen miles distant, with Petya somewhere in the snow between. At all costs, then, he could not wander far from the sheep.

Campolo's warm body brushed against Petya's leg and an idea came to him. It was a slim chance, but it was his only one. In a harsh voice, he ordered the dog to stay where he was. That Campolo would disobey him did not enter Petya's mind. Disobedience was unknown to a sheep-dog. He lived by command alone. Walking carefully so as not to betray his fear, Petya made his way in the direction of the sheep. The hollow sound of a leader's bell was his destination.

When he had gotten into the close-packed bedground, Petya stood stock-still until the sheep had gotten used to his presence. Then he made his way slowly toward the sound of the bell. It was sounding less frequently now, and Petya knew the bellwether was settling down for the night. Petya prayed that the wether would not go to sleep before he found him.

The sound was close now, almost at Petya's feet. This was the moment that could save his life, and Petya stood without moving for what seemed an eternity. Then he bent over and reached his hands out to find the wether. At the first touch of his hand, the animal scrambled to his feet and tried to bolt away. But by then, Petya had sunk his grasping fingers deep into the curled wool. In his fright, the wether twisted and turned in a frantic attempt to escape. Petya threw him on his side and moved his hand upward until he had a firm grip on the wether's collar. The wether's hooves struck out at him, and Petya felt the sharp thrust of them piercing through his pantlegs and into his flesh. He found the wether's head and smashed it into the snow. The wether's struggles diminished to a feeble bleating.

Petya knelt in the snow, gasping from the sudden exertion. When his mind cleared, he knew that he could not hope to keep his grasp on this nearly wild creature throughout the long night. Sooner or later he would doze, and the wether would break free. He debated whether to cut the wether's throat with his knife. But if he did that, the carcass would freeze in an hour and his source of warmth would be gone. Instead, he took off his leather belt, looped one end through the wether's collar, and knotted the other end around his own wrist. Then he lay down beside the wether, burying his freezing hands and face in the thick curled wool.

Fearful that if he ever went to sleep, he would never wake up, Petya fought to keep himself awake. Methodically, he retraced his bewildering journey from the high mountains of the Basque Country to the sights and sounds of Bordeaux. The perfect face and the sad brown eyes of the young girl at Labadiste's hotel had stayed with him, even though he did not know her name. He remembered the interminable clacking of wheels on railroad tracks, the rhythmic clicking of heels on Paris sidewalks, and high-toned city people in city dress. He had felt more at home on the sea, where he could detach himself from his companions and stand alone at the rail looking out upon the endless sweep of water and its ever-changing moods.

New York City had been a nightmare, but after that, the enormous-ness of the plains and mountains during his train ride west had brought him peace. He had not been intimidated in the least by the presence of so much land and so few people. He had felt instead a strange and new sense of expansion within himself.

And he recalled the arrival in Reno and his first sight of cowboys in high-heeled boots, and blanketed Indians, and finally Laborde, the sheepman to whom he would be indentured until he had paid back his passage. Laborde was a Basque who radiated confidence and strength not only from his giant frame but from a square face bronzed and creased by summer sun and winter cold. There was no nonsense in his nature. He rarely smiled, but he had nevertheless been amused at Petya's stubborn insistence that his first wages should be sent back to his grandmother so that she could be buried in a proper dress. In an indefinable way, that had established a bond between them.

Sometime in the night, Petya woke to find that his sheepdog had come to him and lain down against his back. It was as if Campolo had arrived at an understanding of his master's plight. Wedged between the bodies of two animals, Petya began to hope that he would live out the night.

. . . .

"Are you all right?"

The voice poked with little footfalls through the gray cloud in which Petya's consciousness was immersed. Though rough, and strained with care, the sound of that human voice was the sweetest music Petya had ever heard. It was also vaguely familiar; Petya made a great effort to match the voice with a man, but gave it up. He was dimly aware that someone else with some other voice was trying to pry his fingers loose, one by one, from whatever it was they were attached to. Petya forced himself to unravel that mystery first. Then he remembered from a vast distance that one of his hands had been holding onto his own belt, which had somehow become detached from his waist, while the fingers of the other hand were dug like claws into thick fleece. He could not imagine how that could be, and for a while he put that out of his mind, too. But the need to remember seemed important, and with another effort of will he remembered the cold and snow, the blurred world through which he had been stumbling sometime in the past, and, finally, the bellwether and the warmth he had exuded.

But the warmth was no longer there. Sometime in the night the bellwether had died. Petya was immensely sorry. He tried to express his sorrow, but the mumbling motion of his lips cracked them open, painfully, and he gave that up, too, and surrendered himself to the ministrations of his rescuers.

T·H·R·E·E

11

The mood of the day was appropriate for the old woman's funeral. Wintry Pyrenean skies pressed down on bare forests of beech and oak and chestnut. The fields lay fallow, and oxen and sheep, bereft of green grass, nibbled listlessly at hay thrown down from the lofts into their mangers. The windows of the houses were shuttered against the dampness and the cold, and only in the kitchens were there to be found uncertain patches of light from a lamp or a fire smoldering on the grate. Chimney smoke climbed upward in blue wreaths to fuse with the gray of low-hanging clouds.

The ritual of the cortege does not change with time. It was the same when I lived in the village. From the church to the cemetery, the procession moved in cadence to the tolling of the bell. The cortege was led by the priest in a white surplice, intoning the litany for the dead. Behind him walked acolytes in long black cassocks bound at the waist by cinctures. They carried candles that sputtered in the humid air, so they cupped their free hands around the frail flames to keep them from going out.

The casket of Amatchi was borne by the old men of the *quartier*. They were bareheaded, berets tucked into the pockets of their black wool coats and black scarves pinned to their shoulders. The casket was covered with a black pall, and behind it a man carried a black flag with a white skull and crossbones emblazoned upon it. Then came the mourners, the men clad in black and the veiled women in black dresses, black stockings, and black shoes.

Maitia walked side by side with her mother, Jeanne, who held herself aloof and withdrawn. A persistent cough that shook Jeanne's frame did not go unnoticed by the mourners. She shuddered perceptibly every time a breeze caught the black flag with the skull and crossbones, drawing her attention to it. She did not conceal her contempt for the macabre that permeated Basque ritual. To her, displaying such a grim banner made it seem as if the villagers reveled in death. But in her heart, she knew better. The truth of the matter was that they simply did not care much about death. She remembered the wry saying she had heard so many times as a child: "Death means nothing to us. That's life."

Except for Maitia, whose face was shrouded in a meshed black veil, there was not a tear or even a hint of sadness among the mourners in the cortege. They marched stolidly forward, performing a ritual duty.

From the concealment of her veil, Maitia watched her mother and read the open disdain in her posture. Jeanne had not wept once from the moment the news of her mother's death had reached her in Bordeaux. She had come home with Maitia in hand to do what was expected of her.

When Jeanne first got to her ancestral home, her mother's body had already been laid out in the frigid parlor. At least she had been clothed in her best dress, rather than in the nightshirt that was commonly used in order to save the dress for a daughter to wear. Insistence upon the dress for Amatchi had been in Jeanne's tersely worded telegram to the priest, who accepted the demand with the air of one impatient with Jeanne's extravagant city ways.

Jeanne had spent the entire night beside her mother's casket, again because it was expected of her. Because her amatchi's death did mean something to her, Maitia passed the vigil with Jeanne. Chilled through in the stone parlor, Jeanne got up listlessly from her straight-backed chair from time to time to change one of the burning tapers that encircled the casket or to look down upon the old woman's waxen face and hands. In death, Amatchi's face was younger than it had ever been in life, except for the framing of white hair.

As Maitia watched, Jeanne's hand traveled to her own hair. It was already sprinkled with gray.

"Peace at last," Jeanne murmured aloud. "Free from everyone's bidding. Especially *his*." She was silent for a while, and then she said pitilessly to herself, "Well, it was your own doing. You let yourself become a slave for husband and son, intimidated like a frightened little rabbit."

Maitia fixed her eyes upon the floor. She had loved this timid woman who in Maitia's childhood had been the only mother she had known.

· · · ·

Jeanne fixed her eyes upon her father, walking with the men in the segregated cortege. He moved like a stunned ox, staring dumbly ahead, putting one foot in front of the other with a deliberate effort of will. "The light has gone out of him," Jeanne had said to Maitia at homecoming. "He does not have long to live. I can feel no compassion for him."

Whatever love Jeanne had had for her father had been killed with one stroke on the evening of their confrontation about Arnaud.

· · · ·

Seven years had passed since Jeanne had taken Maitia away to live in Bordeaux, punctuated only by visits to the farm at Easter and Christmas. In the beginning, Jeanne had come home to Donibane with her child. Whenever Maitia ventured into the village, Jeanne had felt called upon to accompany her in the role of protector. The precaution was unnecessary. Watching from a little distance, Jeanne saw the warmth with which the villagers greeted her daughter. Gone was the awkwardness that hung over every encounter when Jeanne was at her side. It did not come from hostility, but from a lengthening of the restraint that was always there, as though the villagers were unsure how to interact with Jeanne. They would never descend to being effusive. It was not their way. They were helpless to do anything except escape into an even more distant restraint.

All that had disappeared when Maitia was alone. Shopkeepers stopped with smiles to greet her, and often, Jeanne heard their affectionate name for the girl: Nimignonne, or pretty little one. Then Maitia's playmates from the *quartier* would see her and there would be a flurry of embraces and exclamations over Maitia's new city dress.

Gone were the secret, unpretty smiles of childhood when Jeanne's reappearance had rekindled the flames of scandal.

Jeanne thought back to when she had brought Maitia back to her ancestral home for the first time. Jeanne had looked on in amazement as Maitia, who was not given to demonstrations, threw herself impulsively into her grandfather's arms. Garat's stony countenance had crumbled, and tears had welled up in eyes that no one had ever seen tears in before.

It had been autumn, and Garat and Maitia had gone out hand in hand to see how the orchards and the cornfields were flourishing. He had seated her beside him on the mule-drawn mowing machine that he had bought to cut the hay in the golden fields.

They had come back at sunset, and from the window, Jeanne could see them flushed with color and hear their laughing voices. Theirs was a relationship that Jeanne had never known. For a moment she was hurt at the child's display of open affection, until she realized that Maitia's *aitatchi* was the only father Maitia possessed.

After that, Jeanne's visits to her ancestral house and to the village became fewer and fewer. When Maitia yearned to go home, Jeanne would simply put her on the little train from Bordeaux to Donibane and give the conductor a coin to watch over her until she was safely delivered to what passed for a station at Donibane, there to be picked up and taken home by Garat alone.

·   ·   ·   ·

Through the meshed concealment of her veil, Jeanne appraised the daughter born to her out of the only love she had ever known. With a pang, she realized that the child was child no more. In the seven years since she had taken Maitia away to live with her in Bordeaux, the girl had grown to the threshhold of womanhood. Her bearing was erect and proud. The pride had come early, almost as a defense against her illegitimacy. Her hair had darkened, her features were fine, and her breasts were beginning to bud so that the black silk of the dress she wore fell away from them. Only in her eyes did she show the hurt of the circumstance of her birth. Only in her eyes did Jeanne see the pain that became her own, and in that she resembled Arnaud the last time they had held each other. How often had Jeanne caught her breath when Maitia's eyes had met hers in an unguarded moment.

"Well," thought Jeanne, "that is the cross that Maitia will have to bear, just as I have carried mine. But my cross is not one of guilt. I regret nothing." She looked again at the black plodding figure of her father and thought, "At last you have known loss as I have known it. But you had a life together with my mother, not just the few precious days that I had with the man I loved. And then, too, you have Maitia, who loves you more than she has ever loved anyone. Including me, because you knew her in the only important time, the years of her infancy."

· · · ·

When the funeral was done and Amatchi laid to rest in the family tomb that bore the names of generations of Garat forebears, the mourners paid their calls of obligation at the ancestral house. If they came expecting an elaborate wake of food and drink, they were to be disappointed. Jeanne had drawn the line at that much adherence to custom. What awaited them was cookies and wine. The mourners paid their mumbled regrets, sampled the meager fare, and trooped out again with as much haste as decorum allowed.

Garat was his usual inhospitable self, going off upstairs to change his clothes with the excuse that, funeral or no, the animals had to be taken care of. Jean-Baptiste had taken over then, and Jeanne watched her brother as he assumed a false air of grief and the pomposity of one who posed as master of the household. He was balding prematurely and going to fat, and he shrugged constantly as he met the mourners. Jeanne did not need to be instructed that the lack of a funeral dinner was being laid at her feet.

The village priest was political enough to come into the parlor where Jeanne and Maitia sat in their straight-backed chairs. His commiseration was brief, because he knew that neither Jeanne nor Maitia liked him and he knew the reason why. He was the one who had been responsible for the designation *illégitime* on Maitia's certificate of First Communion. Jeanne treated him with haughty disdain and Maitia raised her unsmiling, unforgiving eyes only once to meet his.

The wake was also the scene of Jeanne's confrontation with the postmistress, who was the town gossip. The postmistress had come to the house so as to have solid foundation for whatever interpretation she chose to make about the bereaved. Maitia greeted her innocently, but Jeanne's eyes, meeting those of the postmistress, saw something she had never noticed before.

This woman knows something that I do not know. It has to do with Arnaud, and I will have it, thought Jeanne. Jeanne's intuition moved her unerringly to a conclusion.

"Tell me, madame," she said. "After I had gone to Argentina, did any more letters arrive for me from the French agricultural specialist?"

The postmistress was caught unprepared by the same tactic she used in her own prying after gossip.

"Why yes," she blurted out. "But your father picked them up for you as he always did."

"Thank you, madame," Jeanne said icily. The postmistress fled the room. It was only by the entrance of another mourner that Jeanne controlled herself. She was filled with loathing for her father, but the knowledge that Arnaud had tried to communicate with her gave her a measure of peace.

Jeanne watched as if from a distance as a young man paid his respects to Maitia. From the exchange, Jeanne gathered vaguely that the young man, whose name was Viktor, had known Maitia from childhood. Jeanne forced herself to pay attention, but she could make no sense out of what was being said. The young man was dressed well enough in a black broadcloth suit that did not look as though it had been handed down. He was passably handsome in a rugged, peasant way, with dark hair and very white teeth. Caught up in the turmoil within herself, Jeanne had time for only one impression. Though Viktor seemed to have manners, there was something elusive in his nature that did not speak of strength.

.   .   .   .

The mourners were gone and Garat had gone to bed after only an omelette and a glass of wine that Maitia had laid out for him. Jean-Baptiste had gone into the village with Chasco, the mayor, on the pretense of assuaging his grief in a tavern. Jeanne was alone with Maitia in the kitchen.

They sat before the great fireplace and its bright, warm blaze. The light from the flames glinted off the old andirons of gray, polished steel and reached up to touch the brass candlesticks on the mantle. From the barn that was attached to the kitchen came the sounds of oxen and sheep settling down for the night. An owl hooted from its perch in the bare limbs of some tree, and another owl answered.

"You know that I have to stay, Maman," said Maitia. "Aitatchi has no one to take care of him now."

The announcement came as no surprise to Jeanne. She stifled the bitterness that surged through her body and stifled the words she wanted to say: *You may stay, but I will never come back to this house until he is dead.*

Almost in a challenge, she said instead, "You know what to expect if you stay here. You will have to cook for him, wash his clothes, take care of all his wants. You'll have to do everything that your amatchi did. It will be no picnic."

"I'm not afraid of work, Maman," said Maitia. "You know that."

"I could pay for a woman to come in," Jeanne said.

"Aitatchi would be miserable," said Maitia. "You know how he hates outsiders to come into the house."

Jeanne seethed in silence, thinking, *I know that only too well!* She breathed deeply and said, "What about Jean-Baptiste? He won't treat you well. He will try to make a slave out of you."

"I'm not afraid of him," said Maitia. "Aitatchi will see that he doesn't take advantage of me."

There was no questioning that. Jeanne was well aware that her father had nothing but contempt for his son. "Well," she sighed in resignation, "you must do what you have to do."

Maitia did not answer, and Jeanne thought, *She is stronger in mind than I am. She may look like Arnaud in her eyes, but inside, she is her grandfather reborn.* In an illuminating instant of premonition, Jeanne realized that Maitia was lost to her forever. *It is my fate,* she thought. *I was born to lose what I love in this world. What is it with me, that I loved so much? Why couldn't I have loved like others love, with caution?*

12

The villagers had long since ceased to be incredulous at the transformation Maitia had wrought in Garat. She had introduced him to all the realms of pleasure he had denied himself throughout his life of toil. He became a fixture at every village fair and feast day and all their accompaniments of dancing and music, games of chance, and competitions in handball and jai-alai.

Maitia had started the process by the simple expedient of hiring a farmhand named Ramon to take care of the animals and do most of the work in the fields. That had been the most difficult thing to accomplish. Garat was not about to give up control of the farm he had worked his lifetime to build. But Maitia had chosen wisely. Instead of a man who might have his own ideas on how the farm should be handled, she had hired one with the strength of a Hercules and mind of an idiot. Ramon did what was demanded of him without question. It was doubtful whether he had ever had a thought of his own since meningitis had taken away most of his brain when he was a child. Ramon was short and heavyset, immensely strong, and almost mute. He seemed immune from sickness, working in damps and cold with nothing to keep him warm except a thin shirt.

Ramon's only fear was of rain or hail. He would run to his little room beside the stable with his hands over his head and emerge a moment later wearing his magic costume, a red stocking cap. On top of that he planted his soiled beret, and then he was protected. He would never set foot in the house, so Maitia brought his meals to him in the little stone shed that contained only a straw pallet, a chair, and a table.

Garat supervised his chores with an eagle eye, telling him precisely what to do each day, and then watched over him to see that the job was done right. But after a year, there was little need for Garat to be with him every minute. Ramon knew what was to be done and worked from dark to dark like an automaton.

Without saying so, Jean-Baptiste welcomed the addition to the household heartily. Ramon could do the work of two men, and such a thing as asking for a day of rest was totally beyond his ken. Jean-Baptiste found even more time to play the bon vivant in the village taverns and at the card tables.

The caring for the garden, the cooking, and the washing were left to Maitia. She accepted the tasks willingly. As her grandmother and mother had done, she joined the women of the *quartier* at the perpetual spring with its roof of blackened tiles and its row of slanting stones set down side by side. The women soaped and scrubbed and slapped their laundry on the stone slabs, rinsing it in the cold water that ran beside the stones.

The first time Maitia went to the perpetual spring, she was met by the women of the *quartier* with puzzlement and distance. They had become accustomed to seeing her with her mother in the elegant dresses of Bordeaux. But Maitia had anticipated them by wearing a plain gray work dress and a long apron and sandals no different from theirs. That and her quiet nature broke down their defenses, and in a short time she was accepted as one of them.

It had cost Maitia no effort at all to fall again under the spell of the Basque countryside. She loved the long winter evenings when the fire sizzled slowly and endlessly because it was made from oak logs chopped neatly to size. She and her grandfather would sit for hours watching the flames dance in the cavern of the fireplace, speaking little and then only when there was something worth talking about.

In the mornings, she was the first in the house to rise reluctantly from the warm haven of a feather bed to shiver in the darkness until she had dressed. The long-burning oak would be in embers, and she would add new chunks of wood and blow them into flames with the ancient hand bellows bearing the pagan sun symbol on its back. After coffee was made, she would throw on a warm shawl of wool to go out to the sounds of morning, the cocks crowing to herald the day. When the hens emerged, the cocks would leap down from their roosts in the leafless limbs of trees and ravish them one by one. She would scatter corn for the chickens and then pause to look down on the village of Donibane below. In the early morning the whitewashed houses and shops with

their patchwork roofs of new red tiles interspersed with the old blackened ones would be wreathed in a blanket of white mist, and only the
tall steeple of the Romanesque church rose through the mist.

When spring came, she would listen to the bleating of newborn lambs
quavering with the morning cold until the sun burned away the mists.
She would listen to the whistling of a neighboring farmer preparing the
land for planting, the notes of trilling purity mingling and competing
with the songs of a hundred birds welcoming the spring.

Then came summer and the brief respite from the work of plowing
and planting; the soft brown earth was readying its yield for the autumn
harvest. It was in these times that Maitia coaxed Garat from the farm to
the feasts and games of village life. She even induced him to go to Mass
on Sundays. She would sit below with the women and children, and
he would join the men on the balconies that had wooden railings worn
smooth by the hands of centuries; and there were those who swore that
his lips moved, at least during the rousing Basque Angelus at the end
of Mass.

·   ·   ·   ·

It had been a full day, and Garat and Maitia were content to sit at a
little table on the fringes of the village square. In the warm, gathering
dusk they watched the festivities of Donibane's feast day wind down to
an end.

The Mass that morning had been impressive. Garat had to admit
that. Greenery had been sown over the cobblestones for the religious
procession that started the day. The priest, clad in his best robes and
followed by his solemn retinue, had carried the monstrance that housed
the sacred Host from the church to the square and back again. Little girls
in white veils had scattered rose petals ahead. During the celebration
of the Mass, men in uniforms of Napoleon's time, tall bearskin helmets
that flashed dazzling light from tiny mirrors attached above the brow,
had stood at attention before the altar. Behind them were the musicians
with their drums and flutes. Dancers with red berets trimmed in gold,
white shirts and trousers, and bells on their leggings stood poised in

the aisles. In the stillness before the consecration of the Host a musician had pierced the silence with a single shrill note from a flute. One drum rattled a staccato. Suddenly a pagan rhythm of flutes and drums was resounding against the stone walls of the church, but at half-time, grave. The uniformed men had raised their spears, and at the signal, the dancers, offering to God that which they held most beautiful, had woven with intricate steps through the aisles to the cadenced half-time of the music. When they faced the altar all sound ceased.

Afterwards Maitia and Garat had enjoyed a long and peaceful lunch in a restaurant, and then walked up the little hill to the fronton that resembled a stone amphitheater. They had watched the young men from half a dozen villages compete at jai-alai. The matches had all been close ones, and Garat had come as near as he could to expressing his admiration at the skill of the white-clad athletes who, wicker *chisteras* strapped to their hands, had propelled the balls with such unbelievable velocity. The memory of one ball lofting impossibly high into the blue sky would remain with him, whose eyes had been fastened to the ground for so long.

When the games were done, there were exhibition dances on the hard-packed clay of the fronton. The spectacle had been heightened by the appearance of a group of tall young dancers, wide shouldered and narrow waisted, from the high mountain province adjoining Basse Navarre. It was the first time they had deigned to make an appearance in the festivities of Donibane, and they had made a memorable impression with their dazzling costumes and the seemingly impossible agility with which they had leaped onto wine-filled goblets without ever spilling a drop. Before and after, they had remained aloof from the local dancers, standing together silently, and hardly exchanging a word with anybody else.

Their aloofness and containment evoked a forgotten memory in Maitia. "I saw one of these from the high province before," she told Garat. "He came out of nowhere to Labadiste's hotel in Bordeaux. He would have little to do with any of the young Basques from the village. I can still see him. He was tall and he had black hair that needed cutting. But he was not unfriendly. He simply wanted to be left alone. My sisters and I laughed at him because his clothes didn't fit and he walked funny. And then I was sorry when I saw him in the kitchen later with the others. He had dignity in his face." She paused, remembering. "They were all on their way to America. I wonder what happened to him there." She looked at her grandfather. "Well, you know, I might even see him there!"

Garat was so startled that he choked on his wine. "What do you mean, *there*?"

Maitia turned her brown eyes full upon him. "But, Aitatchi, I have to consider that. Going to America."

"Why?" Garat asked in anguish.

"What else is there for me to do? I have no expectations, neither here nor in Bordeaux. I have nothing to offer a husband when that time comes."

It was the first time in Garat's life that he found himself in a position of pleading. "I don't want you to go anywhere! I want you to stay *here*."

Maitia reached out and clasped Garat's suddenly trembling hand in her own. "Aitatchi," she said, "I will never leave you. You know that."

A young man was standing by the table. Garat recognized him as a son of the farmer who owned the fields adjoining his own. But Garat had never taken the trouble to find out what the young man's name was.

In a reserved voice Maitia said good evening to him.

"*Gauhun*," the young man said, flashing a white smile. He turned to Garat and nodded his head in greeting. Garat nodded back dourly, but said nothing.

"With your grandfather's permission," said Viktor deferentially.

Garat watched with mingled emotions as the two young people joined the group dancing in the village square, twirling and snapping their fingers. Well, he told himself, she needs to enjoy herself with people of her own age. She has earned the right.

Garat had been more shaken than he would ever admit at the thought of Maitia's leaving him. As far as his own lifetime was concerned, that fear had been put to rest. Maitia would remain with him to the end. But what of the time after that? Maitia running away to a wilderness like America? Garat shivered in the warm, languid dusk. He loved her more deeply than he had ever loved anyone, mother, father, son, daughter, or even wife. But Maitia was right. She had nothing to offer a husband if she remained in the Basque Country. When he died, as inevitably he must, Jean-Baptiste would relegate her to the role of a servant on Garat's own farm. And Labadiste would treat her no better if she returned to the hotel in Bordeaux. When it came Jeanne's turn to die, Maitia would have no expectations there, either.

Garat came to an instant conclusion. As long as he had power to control the future, Maitia would not be tempted to leave for America. She would not want for land or money. Or suitors, for that matter. His eyes searched out the figure of Maitia's partner and appraised him anew. The boy did not have much of the iron strength in his face that Garat prized so highly in his judgment of men. But he was young still, and Maitia could do worse. His muscled body spoke already of heavy labor in the fields. A union between them would provide Maitia with a dependable member of her household.

In the turmoil of his thinking, Garat did not pause for a moment to consider Maitia's wishes in the matter. That was not his way, nor ever had been.

1 3

The afternoon had been still, so that the pine needles hung suspended in lifeless clusters. The wind that heralded the summer storm began to breathe, starting with a long trembling sigh as of a giant coming quietly awake. The pine needles shivered mildly in anticipation, and the insects paused in their droning to listen.

The wind gathered its strength, rising and falling in troubled gasps. It was the sound of a wind wanting to go somewhere.

Campolo was the first to hear. He raised his head from his paws and cocked his ears to the sound. He looked at the man, but the man was still dozing in the high, light sun. The dog allowed the wind to ruffle the shaggy fringe over his eyes for a while, and then he lowered his head to his paws again.

The wind had made up its mind. When finally it was blowing in a steady stream over the Sierra the sheep heard the warning and stirred in their midday rest. Gathering their lambs, they began to move. The sound of bells roused Petya.

Because lately he had taken to dreaming of home, it was a moment before Petya could understand. He lay perfectly still on his bedroll, hearing the wind. Above him, the needle clusters tossed restlessly in their well of blue sky. Seeing them, Petya remembered where he was. He listened for the sheep. The sound of the bells was near. He yawned and stretched. He had not napped too long, after all.

Sitting up on the edge of the bedroll, Petya pushed the fingers of one hand through a tangled mass of hair, and with the other he groped for the makings of a cigarette. When he had smoked it half through, he was awake enough to look around. The burro was contemplating him from the tree where it was tied.

Getting to his feet, Petya stretched again and regarded the mountain above him for the first time. The front of the storm was already licking like ragged edges of blue flame over the rim. Petya's face sobered. He saw the storm with a vague sense of annoyance, as of an obstacle put up in his path at a time when he could afford it the least. He would have to move quickly to reach the place of rendezvous before the storm caught them.

When he approached with the packbags, the burro edged his rump around. Petya sidestepped the halfhearted kick, but before he tightened the cinch, he rubbed the burro's head consolingly. "Be good," he said in English. "We got enough trouble on our hands today."

He sent the burro on his way with a hard slap on his rump. Burdened down by packbags and the bedroll, the burro lumbered into the trail. The big brass bell around his neck clanged noisily. The sound would curb the sheep in their wandering.

Slinging a denim jumper over his shoulder, Petya clamped a beret on his head and pulled it forward so that it jutted over his forehead. He had unearthed it only that morning, as an omen for tomorrow. But now, he missed the sweat-stained Stetson he had so unceremoniously jammed into the clothes sack. The wide brim would have given him protection. He shrugged off his regret, picked up his walking staff and his carbine, and made another cigarette. If there was to be rain, it would be his last smoke for the afternoon.

Sensing the summer storm, the sheep had not ranged widely in their feeding and were spread over both sides of the ravine that sloped down into the trail. Still, bunching them for a drive in the face of an approaching storm would not be an easy thing. Petya raised his head to regard the oncoming clouds. The tattered fringe had already given way to the dark slate underbelly of the storm. There was little time to be lost.

"Go now, Campolo," he said to the dog waiting impatiently at his heels. In a bound, the dog was at full run. For an instant, Petya watched as the dog shot away to skirt the top of the ravine, moving like a shadow through the trees, disappearing and then coming into view again when he leaped over the low clumps of manzanita.

Campolo had been little more than a puppy when Petya and he had gone into the winter deserts together. He was getting to be an old dog now, scarred from too many fights with coyotes, and the near mortal encounter when he had been knocked senseless by a mountain lion. Though the wounds and the too fast wearing down of his body had aged him before his time, a man watching him would not have known it now.

Campolo hardly needed to bark. The aspect of his hurtling approach was enough to send the ewes and lambs tumbling down into the ravine. Hearing the hurried sounds of descent, the sheep on the other slope came quickly into the trail. In a little time, they were bunched and moving with nodding heads upward to the pass.

Campolo had remained on the top ridge. Petya called to him, but the dog stood his ground stubbornly. Petya swore, knowing what the dog meant. Somewhere on the other side of the ridge there was a missing bunch of sheep, and Campolo had cut their tracks.

Petya was tempted to gamble. In all likelihood, the missing sheep would hear the bells of the leaders and come back on their own. But he could not be sure, and the prospect of facing Laborde the next day with a bunch missing made up his mind. He began scrambling up the steep hillside.

When he reached the top of the ridge, Petya stood for a moment to get his breath. Campolo had not been mistaken. The tracks pointed decisively away. "You will find them faster than I," he said to the dog. "Go now, quickly."

Petya had been lucky in his decision. The missing sheep would not have heard the sounds of the main band. They were bunched in a deep hollow of manzanita and rocks, where a black ewe had led them. A quick glance showed twenty head in all. If Laborde had wanted to be tough about it, considering he was out of sorts already, it would have cost Petya.

The black ewe was watching Petya nervously. A troublemaker, she could bolt in the wrong direction in an instant, and then there would be the devil to pay. Beckoning the dog, Petya moved carefully to the far side of the hollow. When he had gained it, he stationed the dog in the escape path and went down to the sheep, making quiet sounds in his throat. The black ewe was reassured. She turned away from him and led the bunch out of the hollow. When they were within hearing of the main band, Petya let loose his anger and set the dog on them. But the sight of their headlong descent down the slope did not please him and he called Campolo back. "You are losing your temper too easily," he told himself. "It's just as well you're leaving."

They had lost precious time. The dark substance of the storm was over them, and the afternoon was filled with blue light. It was not a good sign. This would be no ordinary summer squall. Calling the dog, he began crowding the rear of the band until they were moving up the trail almost at a trot. The sheep went reluctantly. They had already heard the ominous rolls of thunder from the other side of the mountain, and they were unwilling to quit the protecting lee.

When the rain began to fall, Petya slipped into his denim jumper and buttoned it tightly around his neck. The rain was strong, so that it thudded in deep craters in the dust of the trail. The slip of cigarette in the corner of his mouth disintegrated, and he spit out the remains. In a few minutes, he was drenched to the skin. He felt no discomfort. Because this was a testing he could meet with his own weapons, he found himself welcoming what was to come. The storm, at least, spoke a language he could understand.

The pass was a low saddle on the rim of the mountain. It provided easy passage in good weather, but in a storm it was a funnel that drew the heart of the wind and the rain.

Knowing what would happen when the leaders met the fury of the storm, Petya leaped bodily into the rear of the band, waving his arms and shouting at the top of his voice. Shaken by the unnatural sounds, Campolo ripped into the laggards with slashing teeth. Terrified, the band stampeded up the trail.

It was as though the leaders had run into an invisible wall. They came into the top of the pass, met the full force of the storm, and were stopped in their tracks. They milled in confusion, and then they doubled back, only to meet the rush of sheep from behind. In an instant, the pass was transformed into a seething turmoil of collision. But the surge from behind had been enough. The leaders were swept relentlessly over the rim.

When the last of the band had trailed down the other side, Petya let his legs go out from under him. He sat in the mud of the trail, oblivious to the rain that whipped his flesh and a wind that screeched and tore the air out of his open mouth.

After a while, his vision cleared and he could move enough to turn his back to the storm. When he raised his head, it was to see the wind-blasted trees that clung impossibly to life on the crest of the mountain. The trees were like grotesque phantoms of beaten men, with trunks bent wearily against the storm and branches that flailed like desolate arms in the wind, and he was surrounded by them.

Petya was suddenly afraid of a nameless something. Reaching out for the dog, he buried his face in his ruff. The dog stood still on trembling legs, whimpering with worry.

·　·　·　·

In the darkness the sheep had found their own bedground in the aspen grove, without his help. The rain dripped miserably down through the leaves, but the grove was at least a protection from the wind. When he came with the lantern, he saw that some of the ewes had surrendered to the urging of their lambs and settled down in the wet sand. The rest were still standing, too tired to do anything but regard him mutely.

His own strength was spent, and he felt pity for them. "The worst is over," he said. "Lie down with your lambs pressed close to you. At least you have someone with whom to endure the night."

When Petya had unpacked the burro, he had thrown a square of canvas over his shoulders so that it hung like an awkward cape. He threw it back to free his arms, and with the uncertain light of the lantern, found enough dry firewood near the trunks of trees to warm his supper before bed.

He had thrown up the tent against a great pine, so that its trunk would shunt off the force of the wind. It was an invitation to disaster, too, but he would have to gamble on that. As insurance, he threw his axe into the clearing so that its steel would invite lightning away from the tree.

Finding dry tinder under the sodden top layer of pine needles, he made his fire in front of the open flaps of the tent. At first it smoked and almost went out, but then it burst into flame unexpectedly. He piled on the deadwood branches. When he went into the tent, it was to find a welcome surprise. The wind was sliding off the trunk of the great pine in such a way that an occasional gust would make a circle and blow the warmth of the fire inside. He could not have asked for better luck.

Unrolling his bed on the old mattress of pine needles that had served him in other summers, he sat down on it and let warmth come back into his body. There was a dutch oven of beans and bacon in the pack-bag from the night before. Petya considered the trouble it would take to heat them and gave up the idea. He would settle for bread and cheese and wine.

After the first few jets of wine from the goatskin pouch had spread warmingly through his body, Petya gave up the bread and cheese, too. Taking off his clothes, he hung them from the tent pole to dry and got into bed in his underwear. By propping up the clothes sack he used as a pillow, he could both watch the fire and drink from the wine pouch without choking.

By the time the pouch was almost empty, he was drowsy, and a little drunk, too. The rain was falling harder now and the fire was having trouble staying alive. He watched until it had dwindled, and then he sat up and squeezed the rest of the wine from the pouch.

The dog was moving restlessly outside the tent. Before he blew out the lantern, Petya called to him. Campolo thrust his dripping head uncertainly into the tent. "*Chowdi, chowdi,*" Petya beckoned in Basque. "This is one night when you will sleep warm. After I'm gone, you don't have to worry that anybody will make it a habit."

After a while, Campolo settled to lie half in and half out of the tent. He knew the limit of propriety and Petya let it go at that.

The thunder and the scissored lightning had moved on like a noisy vanguard of the storm. But the wind had become stronger. The gusts became blows, hurling the rain against the tent in spattering explosions. Because he was warm and in his bed, Petya could afford to listen to the wind. Its sounds and strengths were like nightmarish music. There was a steady pounding like a drum out of the heart of the wind, and behind it, the deep lion-roaring that was more the sound of fury than strength. The really frightening blows were the ones that struck un-expectedly, like a giant fist coming out of nowhere. When the wind veered, it glanced across the tent in sweeps that made a fading howl as they moved away.

Petya did not mind the strengths of the storm. There was something in them that made a man feel firm and strong. It was the sound of the lost wind that brought shivers to his spine.

This was the wind that rode above all the storm and probed through its weaknesses. Its cry was lost in the roaring, but when there was a lull, it came to him like the high keening of a demented woman. Then suddenly the cry would fade to haunting flute notes that had in them a fearful warning.

Petya turned fitfully in the bed and pulled the rough blankets over his head to shut out the sound of the flute. He felt his courage begin to leave, and the loneliness he most feared welled up from its dark hiding place within him. It was like the first nights alone in the deserts when he had come to America. Though he could never remember having cried in his life, he had cried then.

·   ·   ·   ·

Petya was searching for something. He could not remember exactly what it was, but he knew it was important. He was walking in darkness, enveloped by swirling mists that obscured his vision, and he thought, *Perhaps I am lost.* But it was not that, because he seemed to know where he was going.

The ground beneath his feet was soft with grass and remarkably free of rocks, and it was safe and familiar in a distant, forgotten way. Re-membering that, he also remembered that the ground behind him, over which he had just passed, had not been safe. There had been a preci-pice, and far beneath it, a ledge that jutted out over an abyss. He had been on that ledge only a while ago, and he had climbed from it to the sure ground. He had been dragging something very heavy, but he could not remember what it was. He was not burdened with it now, and he wondered if he had lost it along the way.

He did not want to remember that, because it made him afraid. He reached out to draw closer the canvas cloak he had thrown about his shoulders. His fingers touched the cloak in surprise. It was not canvas after all, but rough wool. Yet, he could distinctly remember throwing the canvas over his shoulders. Had he taken a blanket out of his bed instead? It was a senseless thing to do, but obviously he had done it.

Then, dimly, through a parting in the mists, he saw a tiny gleam of light. Immediately, he was relieved. He had only been searching for his tent, after all, and the fire he had lighted in front of it was showing him the way. He set his steps surely in that direction.

But when he drew near enough to see, he stopped short. The light was not coming from the fire at all. It came from the tiny window of a hut. The hut was made of stone, tiny stones piled one upon the other to make thick walls, and it was very old, so that the roof sagged from the weight of dark slates. He did not need to see that the slates were covered with lichen. He knew the hut too well for that.

But it was absolutely impossible. Ten thousand miles lay between this hut and the land where he was walking. And unless he were in a dream, there could not be another like it in the world.

Well, of course, that was it. He was dreaming. He had been dreaming all along. That was the explanation for everything—the swirling mists, the softness of grass beneath his bare feet, the rough wool cloak about his shoulders. He knew a profound happiness. If only he would not waken before it vanished.

He could not contain his urgency as he approached the hut. Now, the gleam of light in the tiny barred window was an invitation. There would be a warm fire inside the hut, and beside it the old shepherd would be waiting for him. Quietly, because he had been a long time away, he pushed open the low door and ducked through it.

As he had expected, there was a fire burning in the middle of the floor. Its warmth and the familiar smell of wood smoke met him as he stepped inside and pulled the door shut behind him. There was a boy beside the fire. He had gone to sleep sitting down, and his head was resting in his folded arms. He was wrapped in a woolen cloak so that his face was hidden. Yet, there was something vaguely familiar about him. Near the boy, but a little distance from the fire, a man was sleeping. He was lying on a straw pallet, and he was wrapped in a woolen cloak too, so that his face also was hidden.

Neither the man nor the boy seemed to have heard him come into the hut. So as not to waken them, Petya walked softly to the middle of the room and looked about. Everything was as he had recalled it, the packed earth floor, the oaken beams that made the ceiling, the pallets of straw on the sides of the room. Even the mold was there for the making of the cheese, and when he looked closely he saw that it was filled with sheep's milk that was already forming.

He went back to the fire and sat down on the floor opposite the boy. He wished that the boy and the man would wake up. It seemed unnatural that they should not be aware of his presence. He thought about calling to the boy, but for some reason that he could not comprehend, he knew that it would be terribly wrong to do so before it was time. As he sat, he found his attention returning more often to the man. There was something about the still figure wrapped in folds of cloth that disturbed him.

Without warning, the wind came up and went whimpering around the corners of the hut. As it grew stronger, the stone walls seemed first to shake under great hammer blows and then to draw into themselves and shiver when the wind went howling away. He was reminded of another wind he had heard, but he could not recall where it had been. He was cold and he pulled the cloak closer around him.

As quickly as it had sprung up, the wind began to die. In one instant, its roar had filled all his hearing. In the next, it had faded to quavering pipe notes as of a shepherd playing his flute on some lonely rock. Then the piping faded away, too. Suddenly, the night became still as death. And in that moment, he knew at last that the man lying wrapped in woolen folds was the old shepherd, and that he was not sleeping, but dead. The shepherd's body was the burden he had dragged from the ledge above the abyss where the smuggler chieftain had thrown him.

In the stillness, the cries of the little people of superstition who lived in the forest were the anguished cries of despair, like children lost in eternal night. One by one, they had limped out of their hidden caves and were waiting in the mists outside. Petya raised his head to look at the boy. The boy stirred fitfully as the cries pierced his sleep, and then his head flew up. Their gray eyes met across the fire, and Petya knew that he was looking at himself.

14

The first stroke felled Garat as he was coming in from his fields at dusk. He toppled backwards onto the newly plowed earth and stared with open eyes at a sky shot through with clouds as red as flame from the setting sun, unable to comprehend what had happened to him. When he tried to get up, he found that his left leg was useless. He felt the paralysis moving up his left side, and then the realization came to him.

He fell backwards again, his hands clutching at the earth. His left hand would not do his bidding, but with his right hand, he brought a clump of earth to his face and smelled its black richness as though the land that had sustained him for so long would give him strength. When that failed, he gave an inarticulate cry.

Goading the oxen along a new furrow, Ramon heard the cry. He stood for a moment, irritated that something had interrupted his work. Then, shrugging, he laid the goad across the oxen's necks in front of the wooden yoke, and went grudgingly across the field to the prone form that was Garat. Ramon had never been confronted with a situation such as this, and he had never been instructed on how to cope with it.

With a supreme effort of will, Garat mustered speech. "Home!" he croaked. "Carry me home!"

Ramon's brow cleared. Bending down, he picked up Garat as easily as he would a child, and cradling him in his massive arms, carried him to the house. But there he stopped. He had never been inside the house and he had no intention of going in now.

If Maitia had not gone to the door to see why her grandfather was late for supper, Garat would have died in Ramon's arms. She reeled at the sight that met her eyes. It took only an instant for her to recognize the terrible damage the stroke had done. Unable to speak, she motioned Ramon inside with his burden, paused in indecision between the warm kitchen and the stairway, and then pushed him toward the stairway. Ramon mounted reluctantly. Entering the house had been difficult enough for him, but to penetrate the inner sanctum of the upstairs bed-

rooms amounted to sacrilege. Before it was done and Garat had been
deposited on his bed, Maitia had had to scream her orders so that her
intent would penetrate the farmhand's stunted brain.

Maitia covered Garat with a blanket and turned to run downstairs
for cognac. Ramon was blocking the doorway, his beret in his hands.
Maitia turned him bodily around and shoved him down the stairs to the
open doorway. Once he got the idea, Ramon needed no further urging.
He fled out of the door, stood for a moment on the flagstone entry to
breathe a great sigh of relief, and then trudged back to the field to finish
his plowing.

Maitia held Garat's head up while she held the glass of cognac to
his lips. Most of it ran out of one side of Garat's mouth, but the small
amount that trickled down his throat seemed to revive him. He shook
his head as Maitia massaged furiously at the arm that had already taken
on the resiliency of a piece of wood. Garat was trying to speak before
the paralysis could reach his brain and render him speechless. His eyes
were flaring madly, and his face was contorted. Maitia let go of his arm
and tried to understand what he was saying. With his right hand, Garat
was motioning toward the metal box on the stand beside his bed, and
Maitia knew that he wanted her to open it. She did so. All it contained
was a folded piece of parchment. She took it out and tried to put it in
his hand. He waved it away and pointed impatiently to her. Then she
understood that the parchment was meant for her and unfolded it. The
spidery hand script and the official seals swam before her eyes, but the
import of the document did not register in her whirling brain.

The mad flare had gone out of Garat's eyes, and they were peaceful
again. Slurred words spilled from his stiffening lips, and Maitia caught
them. ". . . my will to the notary . . . my land . . . four hundred years . . .
yours . . . care of it . . . promise." Maitia nodded as if she had understood and took Garat's hand in her own. His eyes remained fixed on
hers. They were filled with unconcealed love and welling with the un-
used tears of a lifetime. Then suddenly, a great pain came into them
and his body went rigid in the second and final stroke. Maitia watched
the moist gleam in his eyes film, then glaze. The powerful body gave up

and lay quiet. Maitia leaned to close her grandfather's eyes and laid her
head against his chest. It was then that she permitted herself to cry.

· · · ·

Maitia had been a young woman of no station or wealth or expecta-
tion. In a perverse way, she had been loved and coddled because of
that fact as much as for her beauty and gentle manner. Now, she was a
landowner, the head of a prosperous farm and an ancient and honored
house. She was treated with respect and deference by the shopkeepers,
speculatively by the young men of the village and the farms, and with
a certain apprehension by some of the girls who had once been her
schoolmates. Maitia noticed the subtle changes in her relationships and
they disturbed her. She was not sure which role she liked the most.

Maitia had not had to disclose the terms of the will. Garat was barely
in his tomb before the notary who had drafted his last testament took
care of that. The notary, whose profession imposed a circumspect demeanor, could never be accused of gossip. Whatever he imparted to
others concerning the private affairs of the village were revealed "in
the strictest confidence." But the terms of Garat's will he had kept to
himself. The loosing of Garat's wrath was a consideration to be taken
seriously. Now, however, there were no reins on the notary's tongue and
he related freely to the avid ears of the villagers the startling news.

In the accepted tradition of Basque circumvention of the Napoleonic
code, Garat had named Maitia as his sole beneficiary. The traditional
provision was also made that his son, Jean-Baptiste, was to live on the
property as long as he chose, but that it was left to Maitia's discretion
to determine his income according to the contribution he made to the
work of the farm. As far as his eldest child, Jeanne, was concerned, he
made no provision at all.

Jean-Baptiste had quietly exulted when Maitia's message reached him
at the card table in the back room of the Café Navarre. His father was
dead. The property was now indisputably his. He had calculated with
reason for a long time that his sister Jeanne would never be included
in any will that his father would execute. In Donibane's measure of

things, he would be an important man now, in his own right, free to
spend his time and money as he was inclined. And how long had he
nursed his secret prospect of ridding himself of his sister's bastard? His
mind played now with the pieces of the puzzle that only had to be put
together.

During the three days between Garat's death and his funeral, Maitia
said nothing to Jean-Baptiste about the provisions of the will. But alone
with her mother the day before the funeral she had confided her turmoil. Jeanne looked drawn and haggard, but Maitia put it down to the
death and the approaching ordeal of the next day's rites.

"I don't know how to tell Jean-Baptiste," Maitia said when they were
alone by the hearth in the kitchen. "This property was your birthright,
Maman, and when you renounced it, it should have gone to him."

"Don't think about me," said Jeanne tartly. "I will never be in need
and I want nothing from this place. I never expected or wanted anything from my father." With a bitter look, she said, "I will tell you that I
am amazed that he had the decency to do this for my child." At Maitia's
shocked recoil, Jeanne added quickly, "I know you loved him. But there
are things you don't know. Not now. But when you are through with
your grieving and want to know, I will talk to you."

"But what do I do about Jean-Baptiste?"

Jeanne shook her head. "That I will not interfere with," she said. "You
are a woman of property now. You must make your own decisions."

"I should give him half," said Maitia. "Part of me thinks I should give
it all to him."

"You are out of your mind!" cried Jeanne. "If you share this property
with him, he will destroy it by debt. If you give it to him, he will destroy
you. You made a promise, you told me. A deathbed promise. My father
knew what he was doing. This land was his life."

Maitia's brow furrowed. "But still, I'll be fair with Jean-Baptiste."

"I can imagine how he will treat you when he finds out," Jeanne
had said.

. . . .

Jeanne's prediction was right. Jean-Baptiste learned the provisions of his father's will in the public square. Thunderstruck, he had raced like a madman to the notary's office and had received that man's unctuous confirmation. Beside himself with outrage, he had run all the way up to the *quartier* to confront Maitia.

He found her scattering corn for the chickens outside the kitchen door.

"You twisted him around your finger!" he yelled. "You bitch bastard of a whore and a stinking Frenchman!"

Jean-Baptiste might have gone further with his hands as well as his mouth but the figure of the farmhand had turned the corner of the house and stopped, watching. Ramon did not say a word. He stood with his arms crossed on his Herculean chest. Jean-Baptiste knew in an instant that this mindless brute would hurt him in a most horrible fashion if he touched Maitia. He turned on his heel. As he retraced his steps to the village his body was drenched in cold perspiration.

. . . .

Though the villagers, including his card-playing and drinking companions, saw Jean-Baptiste as a lazy man with delusions of grandeur, he was not a fool. When his anger had cooled and the realization of what he had said to Maitia in his blind rage came home to him, he knew that he was in a precarious position. The truth of the matter was that he had probably thrown away everything, even the slight provision of a house to sleep and eat in. And he would need money to support his habits. How was he to live? In a society where voicing an open insult was unheard of, he had committed the unpardonable sin. He could not conceive how Maitia could ever forgive him. And she had the power now to reduce him to the lowest of stations. He might have to work in the fields alongside that animal of a farmhand. The prospect of that kind of existence was unsupportable. He did not deceive himself that his days would not be filled with sly looks of satisfaction from the villagers. He knew that he was not loved in the village. All the long way down the lane from his home, past the moss-covered ramparts of the Citadel and into the main street of the village, he walked with his head bowed and his eyes downcast, suddenly afraid to look his neighbors in the eye, to return the words of greeting from those he passed along the way.

Uhalde, the pork butcher with the great square face and blond hair, watched Jean-Baptiste pass. He had come out to stand in the gentle afternoon sunshine and visit with Borda, the fabric merchant whose store was next to his.

"Well, Jean-Baptiste finally got what he wasn't counting on," said Uhalde, wiping his hands on his long, blood-stained apron.

The fabric merchant, who had been to Biarritz on a buying trip, had obviously not heard the news. "What has happened now?"

"Old Garat left everything to Nimignonne."

The fabric merchant, who had a fatalistic bent of mind, digested this interesting bit of news for a full moment. "Well, you've got to give Garat credit for consistency."

"No," said the pork butcher. "For good sense." He inclined his head with a jerk toward the Café Navarre, through whose portals Jean-Baptiste had just disappeared. "Those card players would have owned the property, lock and stock, in six months."

"I wonder what Jean-Baptiste will do now," the fabric merchant mused.

"Nothing sensible," said the pork butcher. "That's for sure."

·   ·   ·   ·

In the dim interior of the tavern, Jean-Baptiste brushed past Chasco, the mayor, and found his favorite table in the back of the bar where the sound of the waterfall outside drowned out all but intimate conversation. When he ordered a bottle of vermouth, he did not look up at the tavern-keeper for fear of what his face might reveal. Jean-Baptiste knew

with a sense of panic that soon he would not be able to afford even
vermouth.

Chasco needed only one look at the blotches of color on Jean-
Baptiste's bloated face to understand that he was on the edge of falling
to pieces. He came over and sat down at Jean-Baptiste's table, signaling
to the tavern-keeper for another glass. Jean-Baptiste felt a surge of unfamiliar gratitude that he had at least one friend in the world. He was
so astounded, he had to fight back tears.

Chasco was a short, thickset man in a rumpled suit. He had oily black
hair that fell unkempt onto his white forehead and into his luminous
eyes. His nose was bridged and sharply curved. Chasco had a talent
for making money and a thirst for position. He paid no attention to his
physical appearance, for he had learned early that power came from
money and not from a costume. His natural effusiveness and innate
political sense effectively hid a shrewd and calculating mind.

"I suppose you've heard the news," mumbled Jean-Baptiste.

Chasco felt a genuine sympathy for Jean-Baptiste. They had been
companions in debauchery for a long time, and Chasco knew all of
Jean-Baptiste's weaknesses and understood them because they were his
own. That was what had drawn them together in their secret forays into
seashore Biarritz for weekends of whoring and drinking, away from the
knowing eyes of the village.

They touched glasses. "It was unjust," said Chasco. "I am sorry
for you."

Jean-Baptiste shook his head in defeat. "What am I going to do now?"

"You could go to America."

"And herd sheep like the other dispossessed?"

Chasco was about to say, "At least it might take some of that belly
off you," but thought better of it. "You ought to talk to Nimignonne," he
said instead. "After all, she's very young. She might make a division of
property with you."

"It's too late for that."

"Why?"

Jean-Baptiste told Chasco what he had said to Maitia, leaving out nothing.

Chasco grunted. "You actually called her a bastard?" He shook his head in incredulity. "That wasn't very smart."

"But it's the *truth*," Jean-Baptiste suddenly snarled. "Think of it! A bastard! Sitting on my property!"

The seed of an idea narrowed Chasco's eyes. He muttered, "Let me think. There may be a way."

"What can you do?" Jean-Baptiste said almost accusingly. "The will was signed. And that notary is no friend of yours, or mine." In a dejected tone he added, "And besides, the notary is an honest man."

Chasco bristled. "Give me time. I'll put him under my fist if I need to. He is nothing." The mayor pulled back into the recesses of his mind. "Things may not be as bad as they look."

Jean-Baptiste knew the mayor's power. Only the rich were safe from him, and to them he toadied. They had played the game longer than he, and he knew where not to cross the line. The notary had position, but he had no money.

Glancing around him to make sure nobody was close enough to hear, Chasco whispered to Jean-Baptiste. "This isn't going to be easy. We will have to confront Jeanne Garat, too, and that tigress can undo us. As for Nimignonne, I would advise you to make peace with her at any price. Crawl, if necessary, and I can assure you it is necessary."

Jean-Baptiste was doubtful. "You don't know her. Behind that sweet face is a spine of steel."

"There is also a girl with a good heart," said Chasco. "She can be fooled." He leaned close to Jean-Baptiste. "You are going to mend your ways," he said. "No drinking. No gambling at cards." He turned his thumb down upon the table. "No more Café Navarre." He was silent for a long moment. "No magistrate is going to hand over that valuable property to you the way you are known now. Mend your ways. It's going to be hard work and abstinence for you from now on."

A whimsical thought put a smile on Chasco's lips. "You might even think about getting married. That would prove you've mended your ways." He smiled then with malice. "The girls in Biarritz will miss your company, and so will I."

·   ·   ·   ·

Maitia received Jean-Baptiste's apology with icy distance and contempt for his abjectness. Her instincts and her mother's warning told her not to trust him. But slowly over the days as she watched his show of remorse she realized that she could take no pleasure in seeing her uncle diminished in station and respect. Because she had suffered that humiliation herself, her defenses began to waver. And so she forgave him, telling him in a voice of unconvincing hardness that he would always have a house to live in, and that his share of the farm's profits would be the same as it always had been. Even as she said it, an inner voice told her that she was being a fool, and she almost recanted.

When the lighthearted sound of Viktor's voice hailed the house from the lane, she sighed in relief and forgot Jean-Baptiste. Her pulse quickened, her heart smiled, and she went out into the courtyard to meet him.

Through the open kitchen windows, Jean-Baptiste strained to hear what Viktor and Maitia were talking about. He watched them pass through the gate and into the fields where Ramon was occupied with the spring planting. Jean-Baptiste noticed that Viktor was walking with a new and lordly stride and he swore to himself. *He is already smelling the marriage bed and my land under his feet,* he thought. He felt fear reawakening as he realized that it would be over for him.

Jean-Baptiste went upstairs and sought his bed. Now I am truly undone, he said to himself in despair.

Enclosed by the insularity of the small Basque village that was its own little world, he could not foresee that his dilemma would be altered by forces outside his ken. He could not foresee such a momentous event as the outbreak of a world war and the consequences it would wreak.

F·O·U·R

1 5

The first band of red had begun to outline the jagged rim of the mountain when the solitary doe came down to the green meadow to drink. Above the band of red, the pale arch of a new day moved slowly into a western sky that was still black with night, so that the moon and star at its top shone brilliantly.

The doe had caught the scent of the sheep in the aspen grove and the presence of man, and had moved quietly past them. She had not caught the scent of the old mountain lion who lay hidden upwind in the willows that flanked the meadow. Nevertheless, she knew the spring was located in a dangerous place, and she went down to it with arrested movements of caution.

The mountain lion lay with his scarred head resting on his paws, silent as a stone. He scarcely breathed as the doe planted her hooves in the mud beside the spring, twitching her great ears for sounds in the willow growth. The doe dipped her muzzle into the pool and as quickly raised up again to listen. But the mountain lion had been expecting the ruse and did not move a muscle. When the doe began to drink in earnest, the mountain lion fixed his aim on her shoulders and slowly gathered himself.

The day broke an instant too soon for the old mountain lion. The edge of the sun burst over the rim of the mountain, and immediately there was movement everywhere. A breeze sprang up tremulously, the leaves began to flutter, and there was a tumult of song from a hundred waiting birds. Startled, the doe raised her dripping muzzle from the spring. The mountain lion sprang desperately out of the willow growth, but it was too late. In two great bounds, her slender legs together like a dancer's, the doe was gone. The old mountain lion stood in the spring for a while, and then, glancing balefully at the sky, set off in another direction. In many ways, the mountain lion hated the sun.

Petya paused in filling his canteen to read the story of the tracks at the spring. He saw where the deer had placed her front hooves in the mud to drink, and the cluster of knifed cuts in the meadow grass that showed she had left in a hurry. With his hackles up, Campolo was sniffing at the place in the willow growth where the mountain lion had lain in hiding. Judging the distance, Petya wondered what had intervened to save the deer. It would have had to be something entirely unexpected to thwart such a certain kill. He felt no sympathy whatever for the mountain lion.

When the big canteen was full and he was about to leave, it occurred to Petya that this would be his last chance to drink from the pure spring. He knelt down again and flattened himself to touch his lips to the pool. The water was so cold that he could bear to drink only a few swallows before gasping for air. Still, the taste was enough for remembering.

Now that the time had come to leave this land, Petya realized that he would miss it. When he had first met the new land, it had been as a suspicious and fearful stranger because he did not know what to expect, where the winds came from and what they were capable of doing, what dangers lay hidden beyond the death warning of a rattlesnake concealed somewhere in the sagebrush that surrounded him.

Of the coyotes that stalked his sheep, he cared nothing because they were really no more than dogs. But the first mountain lion he had seen was another matter. There was real danger in those sinews and muscles that rippled beneath the tawny hide. And the first bear he had met standing upright on a moonlit mountain deer trail had made the hair at the back of his neck bristle like a dog's. Instinctively, Petya had not made the mistake of taking a backward step but had veered away from the deer trail and continued his way forward. The bear had watched him pass with a snuffling sound that was almost human, content with the knowledge that he had taught this man to give him a wide berth.

Now, the land was familiar to Petya. The sky above him was washed to a porcelain blue, and raindrops from yesterday's thunderstorm still clung in shimmering beads to the willow leaves. As he knelt by the spring, he heard the clicking of a grasshopper ticking the tempo of an overwound clock, the throaty warble of a songbird, the faint whir of a hummingbird who hung in the air almost close enough to touch. From the willow growth, a blue jay with a lordly crest was watching him. And when he got to his feet, a startled squirrel ran for cover with his tail stretched out behind. All of these he had come to know as well as he had once known the little beasts of the green Pyrenees of home.

On his way back to the camp, Petya regarded a lightning blasted pine tree with fatalism. "Well, my friend," he said aloud. "You caught a good one, didn't you? Your mistake was in getting too big. Didn't you know the lightning always searches out the tallest tree first?"

Hearing the echo of his own voice, Petya checked himself, killing stillborn the rest of what he had to say to the tree. This was one habit he would have to break quickly, before his reentry into the society of people. If anyone heard him, they might think he belonged in the crazy house like so many of the other sheepherders who had ended up there.

But even as he admonished himself, his mind began to stray and he wondered when he had begun talking to the things of nature, his dog, his burro, and even the sheep. It must have come on slowly through the time alone, the long years when the only voice he heard was that of the camptender every two weeks, and then only for a few hours. In the absolute deprivation of days and weeks and months in desert wastes and deep forests, without human company, he had almost lost his iden-tity as a man and had become just another of the creations of nature, joined with them by the only bond they held in common, that of life.

His music had been the sound of the wind, from the sighing breezes of spring to the banshee scream of the winter gale. His comfort had been governed by the brutality of the desert sun that fried his brains and the winter cold that pierced through to his bones. His vistas had ranged from the unfathomable distance of stars in the night sky to the opening of a flower in the morning sun. His sense of time had been marked by the seasons, from the quick drooping death of meadow grasses after the first frost to the incautious blooming of wildflowers in a false spring.

These were the lessons of the new land that Petya had learned. In retrospect, they were easy lessons. Not so the lessons of loneliness. He knew now that no man could remain absolutely alone for too long. Too much aloneness was a living hell, and he had never gotten used to it.

In his first year, he had taken Laborde's advice and stayed away from the town, thereby saving his money. But the next year of aloneness had proved too much to bear. His body had taken on the finished dimensions of a man. In the process, his appetites had, too. He had never known a woman, but from imaginings enriched by the stories of other herders, he yearned for the press of soft, yielding flesh against his body. That, and the ecstasy of the consummation of the act.

In the end, he had surrendered to his hungers and made the fateful decision to go into the town. There, he could not get enough of people. He had clung to every word that any man said until he had sucked him dry of speech. He had gotten drunk, and the sensation of losing himself in a hazy stupor had kept him drunk night after night until his assaulted body had rebelled and he had gotten sicker than he had ever been in his life. And each night, he had gotten himself a whore. He had gotten drunk on flesh until the vast reservoir of his need had run dry.

All that would have been all right, and he could have returned to the winter deserts with some of his savings still intact. But he had gone all the way and tried his inept hand at gambling, too. It was like watching all his wants and dreams dissolve in the pool of money in the middle of the green table. When that had been accomplished, his welcome in the town had run dry along with everything else. And he had gone back to the hills dead broke, as the cowboys liked to say.

On a little sand hill overlooking the camp there was a tamarack that wind and lightning had twisted into the seeming shape of a man. He had seen it first when the morning sun was exactly right and had climbed the hill to see if his senses had been deceiving him.

They had not. If anything, the tree was more provoking close up than from far away. The wind had tortured its two remaining branches into horizontal patterns so that they were outflung like the arms of a man hanging on a cross. Lightning had blasted the trunk so that its crown was bent to one side as if in death, and the exposed roots of the tree tapered into legs that fused into the unburned wood of the trunk. At the base where he had stood was a group of granite boulders, half buried in the sand, that stood like eternal witnesses to pain and sorrow. Altogether, it had been more compelling than any crucifix he had ever seen.

But he never climbed the sand hill again.

· · · ·

The fire from his midmorning meal was in embers, and Petya brought it back to flame. Before putting on the water for his bath, he considered walking to the slope where the sheep were taking their noonday rest, and then gave up the idea. The sheep were content. In the chilly aftermath of the storm they had risen early and fed well on the milk-rich sunflowers throughout the morning hours. They would rest long before moving again.

He was a little apprehensive about the hungry mountain lion. But Campolo was aware of the lion's presence, and he would make his own forays to guard the lambs and alert Petya. Petya glanced at the sun. It was nearly noon. There was barely enough time to get himself ready for Laborde's coming.

While the water warmed, he shook out his blankets and spread them over the manzanita bushes to air. Near the camp, there was a little patch of meadow nourished by a hidden spring. It was in full sunlight. Laying a square of canvas on the grass, he carried his clothes sack and shaving tools to it.

When the water was warm, he knelt on the canvas and washed his face slowly, digging into his ears and the corners of his eyes with rough fingers. When that was done, he propped up the broken mirror and lathered his face until it was covered with white foam. Even though he had stropped the razor to a fine edge, it tugged painfully against the bristles. The first shaving was accompanied by small moans. But the second gave him pleasure. Becoming careless, he managed to nick himself.

He dried his face with the towel and picked up the mirror to inspect the damage closely. Instead, gray eyes met gray eyes in the cracked glass. With a little wave of shock, he remembered his dream, and the dream fused with the reality that had formed it. The leaden feeling took his stomach again as he thought of the letter from home that he had jammed into the packbag. The old shepherd *was* dead. He had been thrown from a precipice. The letter had not needed to spell out the old man's murderer. As long as that smuggler chieftain lived, Petya would be in danger of his own life. "Well, now that I am a man with weapons of my own," Petya said aloud, "I will make it very easy for you to find me." But he was troubled nevertheless.

Emptying out the washbasin, Petya went back to the fire for the rest of the water. Before he took off his old clothes, he laid out clean underwear and a wrinkled but clean shirt, new Levi's, and stockings. Feeling a little foolish as he did so, he peered carefully around in all directions to make sure he was not being watched, and then undressed hurriedly.

Taking the bar of rough soap, he scrubbed himself from head to toe. What was left of the water he poured over his head to wash out the soap. Dripping forlornly, he began to shiver in the high mountain air and dried himself harshly with the scrap of towel. When that was done, he stood for a little to let the sun warm him. Except for the deep bronze of his face and hands, his long-muscled body was as white as the day he was born. He stood like a freshly washed Adam whose extremities had been touched by fire.

The dog watched him with big, liquid eyes that were almost human in their sadness. No, more than human, Petya decided. He had never seen that much sadness in a man's eyes. A man took too much care to conceal that kind of emotion. Petya reached out and took Campolo's head in his two hands and rocked it back and forth with rough tenderness. "We've been through too much together," he said to the dog. "But this time, there is no following me. Don't make it any harder." But the words did nothing to take away the knowledge in Campolo's eyes.

Petya turned his back on the dog so that he would not have to look.

When he was finished dressing, Petya made a cigarette while the sun finished the job of drying his matted hair. Lazing in the warmth, he contemplated his old clothes. They were lying in a tired heap. Purposely, he had worn them until they were in tatters. The sleeves of his shirt contained more holes than cloth, and the Levi's were threadbare at the knees. There was nothing in them to save. And he felt different, too. In discarding the old clothes, it was as if he had cast aside an old body for a new one. But the body was ten years older than it should have been, he reflected wryly.

Petya could not remember much of his last time in town, nor, for that matter, any of his times in town. It was incomprehensible to him how his disasters had happened. The last time when he had gone back to the hills with another year of work washed away as if it had never existed, he had in his remorse blamed everybody and everything. The bartenders had gotten him drunk on bad whiskey. The *palo blanco,* the Spanish pimp, had preyed on a hunger sharpened by too long a time without women. The gamblers had cheated him when he was too drunk to know what he was doing.

His days and his nights had been consumed by violent rages and a desire for vengeance so strong that it could only be satisfied by elaborate plans for killing everyone who had ever caused him harm.

Then one night the truth of the matter came into his tent and lay at his feet like a cold snake. He found himself floundering for his life. He saw the invitation the other lost ones like him must have seen in the glinting metal of the carbine in the firelight. There had been a moment of choice. Then he had picked up the cold snake of truth rather than the carbine and saw himself for the first time with full recognition.

From far away across the mountain, a man's call came fluting up to him. Getting to his feet, Petya sucked the pure thin air deep into his chest and answered the call. He listened until the undulating echoes had faded away. And with that, he thought, I say goodbye to this place and turn my steps toward home.

Campolo stood rigidly erect while the new dog sniffed at him in examination. Campolo's hackles were raised only enough to show, but he was nevertheless ready. There was a steady rumbling in his deep chest.

The new dog could not be quite sure. He was young, with a red ruff like a lion's and a powerful down-tapering body. Still, there was something about the scarred warrior that spoke of much experience in such affairs, and this gave the red dog pause.

Laborde had been watching them with half a mind from where he was sitting on the rolled bulk of Petya's bed. There was a short stick in his hand. "Your dog got old," he said.

Petya and the new herder, Josu, were replenishing the food sacks from the provisions that had been brought up on the packhorse. "Sure he got old," said Petya.

The red dog had made his decision. He was standing shoulder to shoulder with Campolo. Each was waiting for the other to make the first move. Laborde threw his stick. It struck the red dog solidly on his hind end. The red dog yelped and slunk away. Campolo turned his back on him and came to the edge of the camp to sit down.

"He's nearly too old for work," said Laborde. "I don't know what I'm going to do with him."

"He's willing," said Petya curtly. "I never saw such a dog for work."

Laborde shrugged dispassionately. With prosperity he had begun to go to fat. There was a new Stetson with a narrow brim tipped back on his head, showing his gray hair. Despite his Levi's, he had worn expensive button shoes on the horseback trip to the camp. The soft brown leather and the knobby buttoned toes were covered with a film of dust.

"Maybe I'll take him home to the ranch for the kids," he said. "That will put him to some use. It doesn't matter if he gets ruined, now that you're going home to be a hero."

There was an edge in Laborde's voice, but Petya pretended indifference. Better the spoiling of children for Campolo than a bullet. Flipping a knot into the sugar sack, he tossed it into its proper place in the packbag. "That does the job, Josu," he said to the new herder. "Looks like you got everything."

"Everything and five pounds of garlic," Laborde said dryly.

Josu acted as if he had not heard. The little eyes in the wizened face darted around the camp until they found Petya's worn walking staff. Picking it up, Josu went off through the trees to bring the sheep back for the last count. The red dog followed him. After a moment of hesitation, so did Campolo.

"Why did you bring *him*?" said Petya.

"Because there was no one else to be found," said Laborde. "That goddamned war over there has cut off all the herders. The Germans are torpedoing the hell out of the French boats."

Petya ignored the innuendo in Laborde's words. "As long as Josu has got his garlic soup, he'll be all right. A man would have to be dead not to get fat lambs out of this feed."

"He might as well be dead as crazy," said Laborde, unwilling to let it go. "And I will be the one to pay for it at market."

Petya busied himself blowing the fire back into flame. With success, Laborde was becoming intolerant, too. What had happened to Josu was a thing that a sheepman should understand best. There had been a day in Josu's life when he realized he was losing his mind. In the last moments of sanity left to him, he had seized upon an old wives' story from home and had devoured great quantities of garlic to save himself. He had lost his mind anyway. The one idea left to him was that of garlic soup, and he made it his fare morning, noon, and night with the singleness of mind that only a crazy man could muster.

"You're not being fair with me," said Laborde, regarding Petya with Basque contempt for those who fail their duty. "And you're not doing your name any good, either, quitting the sheep before the lambs are shipped."

"You have no complaints," Petya flared. "I've been out here five years this time without once going to town." He added in a deliberate lie, "Anyway, you know the French have conscripted me."

"*Merde,*" said Laborde. "They can't conscript you. You're an American citizen." Laborde, anticipating the coming war in Europe, had made sure that his herders took out naturalization papers as soon as they had learned English well enough to pass the test.

"You read the letter," Petya said. "To them it doesn't matter if I'm an American citizen."

"The French can't have you deported from this country."

"No, and they can't stop me from going home, either."

"*This* is your country!" said Laborde. "Who are you trying to kid? The French treat us like turds. They always have and they always will."

"What about my family?" asked Petya. "I don't want the Germans taking over my home."

"Oh, my God!" cried Laborde. "Do you think the Germans care about our poor little provinces? Even if they win, what do you think will happen? Absolutely nothing. The politicians will make an armistice, everybody will go home, and nothing will have changed. The only ones who win in any war are the bastards who make the cannons to kill the kids."

"All the same," muttered Petya. "I'm going home."

Laborde shook his head in near despair. "Listen to me, Petya," he pleaded. "I'm wiser in these things than you are. You will never see your home. The French will put a uniform on you and send you to the trenches and that is all you will ever see of France, much less the Basque Country. Because you will sure as hell be killed. They are slaughtering each other over there."

As Petya put the blackened coffeepot back on the fire, Laborde's eyes narrowed. Petya's hand was trembling. Laborde glanced sharply at his tight profile. My God, he thought. That's the reason he's going back to France. I've left him too long alone. He is losing his mind. He'll use any excuse to get out of these hills. It's not the war at all. Laborde's thinking probed. What he's really afraid of is the town. He can't stay here anymore without going crazy and he's afraid of losing another five years of his life if he goes to the town. What should I do?

The sound of bells had been drawing closer, and the sheep were trailing into the flat where the obligatory counting would be done. Getting up with an effort, Laborde went to the edge of the camp to watch the leaders come in. When he stood up, his rounded stomach protruded over the top of his Levi's.

Laborde came back to the fire and took the cup of strong coffee Petya had poured for him. "The sheep look good," said Laborde with gruff kindness. "It's a shame you can't see them through the rest of the summer."

Before he could contain himself, Petya blurted out, "I'm getting out of Reno before the other herders get there." His voice trailed off. "That's where I've made my mistake. Everybody in town together. Everybody with lots of money. Everybody wanting to have a good time, including me."

Laborde regarded the brown liquid in his tin cup. "It's too easy, Petya. Thinking you can miss all that by going to town now. It doesn't matter when a man goes to town. The town is the town. You can't change that."

"Don't worry," said Petya. "I'll keep my money this time all right. This time I will take it home with me."

In an instant of decision, Laborde said, "If you change your mind . . ."

Petya did not hear him out. "It's different for you," he said passionately. "You've made your success in America. Wife and family and friends and ranches and a house in town. What do I know of such things? What I know of America is no more than a coyote knows."

Laborde had long ago quit giving advice to any man. They would listen for a minute and just as quickly forget. His words might change a man's thinking for a day, but as soon as he turned around, that mind would return to the set routine of its ordained pattern. There was no altering a man's fate. At best, there was only a postponing. Yet, he could not help being troubled. Laborde realized suddenly that he had grown fond of this young herder.

Then Laborde reminded himself sternly that sometimes there *could* be an altering of fate. He was remembering the gambling and how bad it had been for himself. The years when he hadn't even gotten past the poker games at the shipping corrals, the times when he had lost all his wages and gone back to the camps without even getting to town. And the one time that had broken it, when he had gotten into an argument with the foreman, and the foreman had said in derision to the Scotsman who owned the outfit, "Laborde has worked for us five years and he owes us five dollars. What do you want to do about him?" And the Scotsman had laughed and said, "Well, we can't let him go owing us money. We may as well keep him on."

Listening to that exchange had given Laborde a sudden cold perspective on his life. He quit gambling and saved every cent for the time when he could own his own outfit. The servitude was long, but Laborde's day had finally come.

Then, long afterwards, there had come another day when he was on a trip to buy ewes and he had gotten too drunk in a bar with the other sheepmen, all rich like himself. He had thought, What is a little poker game when you can afford to lose?

He had found out what a little poker game was. The game had gone on all that night, another day, and another night. By the time the second night came around, Laborde had lost the money he had in the bank, he had lost his sheep, he had lost his range, and he had lost the house in town where his wife and children were sleeping at that very moment. The only thing left was the car he had driven to town in. And when he put that up, they had all gone out with flashlights to get the serial number off the car. But that had changed his luck, too. He won that bet, and he won the rest of them. By the end of the night, he had won back everything he had lost, and five hundred lambs to boot.

Laborde had thought that was pretty funny about the five hundred lambs to boot and was laughing to himself about it as he drove home the next day. Then the realization of what he had almost done to his life and his family came to him. He had had to stop the car because he was shaking too much to drive.

· · · ·

His sheep were coming into the flat for the counting, leaping as though clearing a fence as they passed in front of him. After the first thousand had passed and he could feel the weight of ten stones in his pocket, Laborde began to feel secure again. And he had made his decision.

"How much money you got in the bank?" asked Laborde.

"You ought to know," said Petya. "You put it there."

"Subtracting your clothes and tobacco, five thousand dollars then," said Laborde. "If you change your mind, I'll make you a deal. This band of sheep for your dollars."

Petya cut him off abruptly. "I've told you. I'm not changing my mind."

"You don't understand what I'm trying to tell you," said Laborde in exasperation. "I'm willing to make you my partner."

Petya stared at him, too dumbfounded to utter a word. Anger began to flare again in his eyes.

"Not a full partner this minute," Laborde said quickly. "Not this year. Maybe not for a couple of years. But when you have shown me you can come back from the town with money in your pockets, when you have shown me you can handle the sheep business the American way, then we'll talk partners." He paused, wondering if he were overbuilding his case. "It's not a picnic, you know, fighting for land and water. Worrying yourself to death about the price of wool and mutton. You have a lot to learn. But you know the land now and you know the sheep. Everything starts there."

Petya was unsure of his ground. "But I want to go home."

"You don't," said Laborde wearily. "What you want is to get out of these hills." He nodded toward Josu. "Before that catches up to you."

His mind whirling, Petya fixed his eyes on the ground so that Laborde could not see the fear that he knew would reveal itself there. But Laborde had read his mind.

"Will you do me one favor?" he said.

Petya's voice was hoarse. "What?"

"When you get to town," said Laborde, "stay at the 'priest's' hotel. Visit with your friends and get a little drunk. But not so drunk you can't face me in the morning. Find a clean whore and stay with her half the night. But not all night and not with all your wages on you. Just enough and no more. Then go see that little shit of a French consul. Then come see me before you promise him anything. *Anything!*"

"I *will* get drunk," said Petya as if he were speaking to himself. "The rest of it is none of your business."

·   ·   ·   ·

When the sheep were counted, Laborde and Petya descended the near side of the mountain on horseback. They paused at a vantage point from which they could see the sweep of hundreds of miles of desert and mountain ranges that lay one after the other until they faded into one in the haze of distance.

Petya looked back. His tent under the great pine was a tiny white pyramid of familiar shelter. There was smoke wisping up from the fire, and Josu was bent over the flame. Nearby, the red dog sat on his haunches and watched the man. The sheep were settling down for the night and Petya could hear the delicate sound of bells. Above it all loomed the tree with outflung arms, raised up on its mound of white sand and looking down with compassion on the little figure of a man who had stayed too long alone in the mountains.

16

At nineteen Maitia's half brother Michel was tall and slender. His thoughtful gray eyes were set in a fine-boned face that would have been called delicate except for the military moustache that nearly every French soldier affected. That and the tailored uniform of an officer had caused a fluttering of hearts among the girls at Donibane. The mystic attraction of war-doomed masculinity fanned flames of patriotism for France that had never before been felt in the Basque village.

In the years Maitia and Michel were growing up together in Bordeaux, how often had Michel's normally serious expression broken into radiant amusement at one of Maitia's wry tales about her village. The sound of his laughter would break against the formal stiffness of the ordered household so that his mother and sisters would start in wonder. A frown would cross Marie-Claire's face and a hurt come into the eyes of gentle Madeleine. Between their brother and their half sister there was a relationship they did not share. Although they accepted Maitia with genuine affection, there hovered between them an indefinable distance that would not be bridged, a distance that had never existed between Maitia and Michel. They would often finish each other's sentences. A secret word, a signal by glance or gesture would provoke in the other a smile, a lifted eyebrow, or a resigned droop of mouth and shoulder.

Maitia's happiness and pride in Michel's visit had been tempered by his serious demeanor. It was the first visit Michel had ever made to the farm at Donibane. That, Labadiste had prevented out of his stubborn insistence that the earth of the fields would never soil the hands of his only son.

Beneath her brother's urbane exterior, Maitia knew that he was concealing something. She felt his preoccupation and the shadow fell on her own senses.

· · · ·

Through the open window of the kitchen that gave onto the paved terrace, Maitia could hear Michel and Viktor talking. From the low and serious tones of their voices, she knew they were talking about the war, and it filled her with apprehension.

Maitia had spent the morning preparing the noon meal. The occasion would mark the first time she had invited Viktor into her household. Their courtship had been circumspect in every way. Sobered by the knowledge of how passionate love and secret trysts had rained disaster upon her mother, Maitia had made sure that she and Viktor were together only in public places on market days and festivals. Their walks in the country lanes were always in full view of the farmhouses that bordered their way. Her only slight bending of propriety had been in offering Viktor a glass of wine in her open courtyard after he had passed an afternoon helping Ramon in the fields.

When Jean-Baptiste had offered to help with the farm, Maitia had been shocked. After watching him, the surprise had turned to despair. Jean-Baptiste was useless. If the farm had relied on his inept and careless control, it would have been reduced to a shambles in spite of the farmhand's animal toil. Maitia had come to rely more and more on Viktor for help.

Maitia had convinced herself that she loved Viktor. They had never kissed. They had never embraced. And Viktor never pressed. He treated her with studied respect. He knew that her passion for respectability had wrapped her round with an invisible shield, and he knew that that passion would kill any other that could ever tempt her. Viktor accepted this as a matter of fact. His own passions could be satisfied elsewhere. And Maitia had responded to Viktor's attentions by opening a lonely heart to him.

Now, watching Viktor and her brother together on the terrace, she marveled at how different they were. Viktor was leaning forward in his chair in his Basque way, his elbows planted on his knees and his work-hardened hands clasped in front of him. The broadcloth coat he wore was stretched tight by the thick muscles of his back. The unfamiliar necktie constricted his throat so that from time to time he tugged unconsciously at his shirt collar. His skin glowed from his exposure to sun and air, and deep creases were etching themselves around his eyes.

In contrast, Michel was the educated product of his protected city upbringing. His slender form was relaxed in his chair, his knees were crossed in casual fashion, and his hands that had never known manual work were slender and unblemished. He had not been formed to be a soldier, but that had not been able to prevent his becoming one.

With a sudden shadow of fear, Maitia thought to herself, *He is not the kind that should go to war.* She could not accept the image of her brother existing in the filth of the trenches or of his actually shooting at another human being. Then she thought, with an easing of her fear, that it would not really happen. Michel would not really go to war. Labadiste had used his influence to have Michel posted to a command office close to Bordeaux, far away from the front.

Throughout the noon meal, Viktor had eyed Michel's uniform with mixed emotions playing over his expression, contempt and admiration vying for dominance. Now she listened uninhibited to their conversation.

"It's strange, don't you think?" Viktor was asking sarcastically. "The French never noticed before that we existed. They didn't consider us part of their France. Now that they need us, they conscript our men— my own two brothers! If anyone resists he is arrested as a deserter." He lowered his voice to a confidential tone. "You wouldn't believe how many have crossed the frontier into Spain rather than fight for the French."

"I am trying to understand," said Michel quietly, "but I don't. I know so little about the Basques. My mother never talks about her childhood. And my father is ashamed of his Basque blood. I was raised more French than Basque."

Viktor pondered Michel's candor. "I will tell you the truth then, too," he said heavily. "I would go to the war, if I could. Better the French pushing us around than *les boches*."

"Why don't you enlist?"

"They took my older brothers," said Viktor. "It is my responsibility to stay on the property and to work my father's land. I have no choice."

"The army needs food as much as bullets," Michel said tactfully.

Maitia had come out onto the terrace. "If it weren't for Viktor," she said, "this farm would not have survived. He does the work of two men, on his father's farm and on mine. He's doing as much as any soldier."

"What about our uncle?" asked Michel. "He's too old for the army. Doesn't he help?"

When Maitia said nothing, Viktor answered for her.

With a feigned sigh of resignation, he said, "He does nothing. Now that his true talents for drinking and gambling have been forsaken, he doesn't do anything."

Michel bridled. "If it's the Basque way to talk about other people's relatives, I don't like it."

Viktor shrugged. "I have the right. Maitia will be my wife. I don't mind helping here because I am protecting my investment."

Michel barely managed to conceal his distaste for Viktor's callous statement of fact. *He displays the sensitivity of a stone,* he thought. Aloud he said with cold politeness, "Take care of Maitia. She is my beloved sister."

· · · ·

In the evening when Michel and Maitia were alone by the fire, he said to her, "So you are really going to marry that man?"

Maitia nodded.

"But you're not in love with him!"

Maitia said simply, "I don't know what a woman in love feels like. Maman did. And I don't want it. It brought her nothing but heartbreak."

"Memories, too," said Michel. "I can see it in her eyes when *he's* not around."

"You're a romantic," said Maitia. "Anyway, I think I love Viktor. Not in love. Love. He's a hard worker. He'll make something valuable out of this property."

"A marriage for practicality?" Michel asked in disbelief.

"You really don't know the Basques, do you?" she said. "A marriage of convenience is the only kind of marriage that is looked upon with favor here. You know what to expect of each other."

Michel's eyebrows lifted quizzically. "No love in a Basque marriage?"

"It's not considered important," Maitia said.

"Poor Maman," said Michel softly. Then, in another tone, "Poor Maman."

The image of her mother's drawn and listless face resurfaced in Maitia's mind and she asked in sudden concern, "How is she, Michel?"

Michel looked at his feet. "Not well. The hotel is full of soldiers and *he* is making a lot of money. *She* is working too hard."

Maitia felt a growing alarm. "What are you trying to tell me?"

Michel raised his head and looked evenly into Maitia's eyes. "Our mother is sick."

"Very sick?" Maitia managed to whisper.

Michel nodded. "She has consumption."

Maitia's eyes widened in terrible comprehension. "Is she going to die?"

"Not today. Not tomorrow," said Michel. "Don't ask me about next month."

"I must go to her," Maitia said in a daze.

"Yes," said Michel. "She wants you."

Maitia was caught in a rising tide of anxiety.

"You're in Bordeaux, aren't you? You're stationed where you can see her?"

Michel was silent for a long moment. "Don't you even suspect why I've come to see you?"

She looked at him, panic beginning to take hold.

Michel said quietly, "I'm going to the front."

Maitia rose to her feet and regarded him with fury. "Not now! Not now, when Maman is dying!"

"My comrades are there in the fighting. In their eyes I am a coward."

"You're not!" she shouted.

"No, I am not. The only cowardice I ever had was when I didn't stand up to my father. Well, that's over with, thank God!"

She stared at him. "What have you done?"

"I confronted him. I told him I had gotten my orders changed. He disowned me."

Maitia was stunned. "How could he?"

"I was disloyal to him, he said."

Tears were streaming onto Maitia's face. "Don't go, Michel. Don't go. You can still change it! Labadiste will change it!"

Michel shrugged. "Well, what's the loss," he said. "We never got along anyway. I could never have worked under his thumb."

Michel stared into the dying fire in the grate. Then he got up and put an arm around his sister. "Maitia, dear Maitia. I will survive this war. I know that as surely as I know that I will never look on my father's face again. And I am glad for both."

Maitia pleaded, "Michel. Wait a little while. We will go to Bordeaux together."

"I can't. I leave tomorrow."

Maitia wept then, her head against the soft wool of her brother's tunic. He held her gently and the strong beat of his heart resounded against her own. Maitia held onto the moment, knowing its imprint would have to last her lifetime. Finally she straightened, put both hands on his shoulders, looked long into his eyes, and kissed him quietly on both cheeks.

·   ·   ·   ·

When Michel had gone to bed, Maitia went outside and sat on the stone bench in front of the house. The scent of fresh-cut hay mingled with the barnyard smells and the bittersweet decay of autumn leaves. They had never seemed so poignant and so dear. And so suddenly elusive. Maitia felt as if the support of house and land beneath her feet was crumbling. Something was going to be wrong. Something was going to be dreadfully wrong.

17

A newsboy with floppy hat and knickers was standing on the curb of Second and Virginia, the main intersection in Reno. A stack of newspapers was stuffed into a canvas bag that looped over his shoulder and across his chest.

It was late afternoon and the newsboy was caught up in a wave of men that streamed out of the vaulted doors of a bank. The gold lettering on the doors said First National Bank of Nevada, and the men who emerged from the building were dressed almost exactly alike in high white collars and neckties and business suits.

Virginia Street, down which Laborde's Cadillac had come, was the Americans' street, lined with ornate bank buildings, buildings that housed business and law offices, an arcade of clothing stores, a sprinkling of barbershops, and a great number of saloons with gilded double doors.

The wave of men that had come out of the bank building dispersed when it reached the sidewalk. Some went into barbershops, but the greatest number trooped into the saloons for a drink or two before walking home to elm-shaded back streets with imposing brick homes and sweeping lawns, and to white frame houses with neat little lawns and flower gardens and white picket fences.

The newsboy did a flourishing business until the wave of suited men receded. When Laborde's square black Cadillac slowed and stopped at the intersection, the newsboy stepped off the curb and thrust a *Gazette* in front of Petya's face. Startled, Petya looked wildly at Laborde. Moving the gear shift to neutral, Laborde dug into his Levi's pocket for a coin. He found a quarter and leaned past Petya to give it to the newsboy. "Keep the change," he said. The newsboy looked at the coin in his palm and his face broke into a tightly exultant smile. Laborde waved this thanks aside and engaged the gear, glancing at Petya as he did so.

The tension had been building in the young herder all the long way from Laborde's home ranch in the foothills down dusty desert roads that led to the new, paved highway to Reno. Petya's eyes stared fixedly forward. The muscles of his face were drawn as taut as violin strings over his high cheekbones and finely bridged nose. A pallor lying just below the surface had begun to whiten skin bronzed by the high mountain sun. My God, thought Laborde. He's more like a scared animal than a man. Then Laborde reminded himself that it had been five years since Petya had seen civilization.

When the late-day tangle of cars and horse-drawn buggies and freight wagons had thinned enough for him to pass through, Laborde turned his Cadillac off Virginia Street and made his way east to Lake Street, which was neither paved nor elegant nor shaded. This was the street of the foreigners, and it knew no distinctions of class. It was a street of Italian hotels, Spanish hotels, Basque hotels, Jewish clothing stores and Jewish pawnshops, Chinese laundries, and shabby, hole-in-the-wall restaurants of a dozen nationalities, all crammed together in no discernible pattern.

Laborde braked the car to a stop in front of a two-story hotel with an unpretentious front, a scarred and unnecessary sign that jutted out over the street with the help of wires, double front doors, and little curtained windows upstairs where sheepherders, cowboys, prospectors, and ranch hands stayed during their times off. Before the time of the foreigners the building had been a western speakeasy with a high, polished bar and a lone chandelier hanging from the patterned tin ceiling. Both the bar and the chandelier remained as a legacy from better days.

Petya heaved his bedroll and the cardboard suitcase that contained his town clothes out onto the sidewalk. Reaching into his back pocket, Laborde pulled out a battered wallet. "Here's spending money for you," he said brusquely, peeling off bills from a thick wad of money. "If you need more, get it from the 'priest.'"

"I don't need that much money," Petya protested.

"Then guard it well," said Laborde, and Petya knew he was being tested.

The double doors of the hotel opened and the "priest" came out to meet them. The proprietor, whose name was St. Martin, was a tall man with sad eyes. Laborde said to him, "Early customer for you. Take care of him."

St. Martin raised his eyebrows slightly. "Is he sick?"

"No," said Laborde. "He's a patriot."

St. Martin shrugged and picked up the suitcase, leaving the bedroll for Petya to carry. A patient man, he had decided that time would tell him what Laborde was talking about.

St. Martin had never really been a priest. He had run away from seminary to come to America, defying the Church and his family. But to the Basques, having been in seminary amounted to the same thing as being a priest. That, and the fact that St. Martin looked like a priest. Even though his hair was full in front, there was a perfectly round bald spot in back, and it was said he had been visited with a tonsure to teach him a lesson. St. Martin might have heard the story and the fact that his customers called him "priest," but if he had, he never talked about it. And if he felt any guilt about running away from seminary, he did not speak about that, either.

Although St. Martin was an innkeeper, he regarded his little hotel as a place of shelter within the bounds of making a living for himself. He served drinks to the young herders, but when they showed signs of getting drunk he reasoned with them to go to bed. He allowed the *palos blancos*, the pimps of Lake Street, to come into his hotel for a drink or a meal, but he forewarned them that there would be no surreptitious slipping of room keys to his innocents. In these matters, however, he was not altogether successful.

For the old herders who did not come to town for redemption, he cared nothing. They could drink and whore and gamble without fear of his disapproval. As far as St. Martin was concerned, they were lost souls anyway. The one concession he granted them was credit when their money was gone. This was only because they were Basques, after all, and would get around to paying him back when they could. This had proved to be an accepted fact in St. Martin's dealing with old herders, and besides they had enough sense to guard their credit against the next time they came to town.

The young herders were another matter. St. Martin looked upon them as waifs in the American wilderness and he saw himself as their protector. "Country of strangers, country of wolves," he would intone to them. He repeated it so often that it became another nickname for him, behind his back.

The young herders, who had never seen one hundred dollars in cash money in their lives, went into the deserts and the mountains and came back at the end of the sheep year not only with a hundred dollars, but with a thousand dollars, and for them it might as well have been a million dollars. They could not conceive that it was possible to spend that much money. Most of them found out in a hurry that it was very easy to spend that much.

Petya shouldered his bulky bedroll and St. Martin took the suitcase, leading the way through a side door. At the landing to the narrow staircase, St. Martin said, "No need to carry your blankets upstairs. Joe can put your bedroll in the cellar. The exercise will do him good. Or kill him," he added with contempt in his voice for the old sheepherder who earned his keep and whiskey by washing dishes and cleaning up the saloon.

Petya let the bedroll slip to the floor and followed St. Martin up the stairs. St. Martin stopped as though thinking, and then opened the door to a room that faced on the alley next to another little hotel. The room was stifling and airless. St. Martin set Petya's suitcase down and opened the windows. The barest flutter of late afternoon breeze wafted through the threadbare curtains. St. Martin surveyed the room to see if everything was in place. He did not need to look very hard. The room contained an iron bed, a single chair, and a chest of drawers with a water pitcher and washbowl on top of it. St. Martin looked into the water pitcher. "It's fresh enough for washing," he said, and went to the door.

He was about to close the door when he paused. He had been appraising Petya quietly. In the five years Petya had stayed away from town, he had changed. His shoulders and arms had filled out. The long face, bronzed now with sun and wind, had chiseled down into the face of a man.

When he wanted to size up a man, St. Martin looked at his eyes and his mouth. That was where a man revealed what he was made of. In Petya's level gray eyes, St. Martin saw the wariness of a coyote; and in the grim set of the lips, he saw a mouth that had forgotten how to smile.

"You look like someone who's got his mind made up," said St. Martin.

"I got my mind made up, all right," Petya said.

Petya was not quite successful in concealing from St. Martin's practiced ear the seeds of indecision in his voice.

"Do you want to tell me about it?" said St. Martin.

"No."

"Dinner at six," said St. Martin and closed the door.

. . . .

Not that it made any difference, because he would not have wasted the money on a new one anyway, but the suit was still a fair fit. Petya had broadened some in the shoulders and his arms seemed to have grown longer, but if he kept them close to his sides the wrists did not protrude too much. About his hands, there was frankly nothing to do. They were rough and hard as boards. But what the hell, Petya thought. No one will be looking at them anyway.

The only thing he found troublesome was the necktie. He debated about going down to dinner without it, but gave up the idea. For the first night, at least, it would not be seemly. He would just have to endure the constriction.

He sat down gingerly on the massive iron bed, being careful not to wrinkle the coverlet too much. He was restless, and he missed the pocket watch that could tell him how near dinnertime was. He had had a watch once, and a town hat, too. The watch he had pawned the last time, and as for the hat, he never knew what became of it. He would have to buy both of them new tomorrow.

Making a cigarette, he absorbed himself in the play of smoke in the small room. It hung in the air as heavily as the silence of confinement. He began toying idly with the thought of going downstairs to find out what time it was, and as quickly put it out of his mind. To do so would mean wasting money in the saloon. It was best to stay where he was. St. Martin would certainly send someone up to tell him that dinner was on the table.

Outside he could hear the muted sounds of traffic, the swirling city sounds that carried to his ears as though through water. But how quiet it was in the room. He could not associate that with the other times. But of course it had always been autumn then and the lambs shipped to market. The hotels had been filled to the brim with a hundred sheep-herders and cowboys taking their time off in town. The saloons were blue with tobacco smoke and deafening with a babble of Basque and Spanish, French and Italian, and the English running through it that served as the common language for all. Sheepherders and cowboys were swapping stories and exchanging complaints about their bosses, sheep-men lamb buyers cemented their bargains with whiskey, gamblers chose their victims with care, and the pimps were slipping hotel-room keys to the willing.

Petya felt the stirrings of vague excitement. In one way, he would have liked to see all of that one last time. Then he remembered the consequences of one last time. Petya got up and crossed to the window and parted the threadbare curtains. Across the alley, barely twenty feet away, there was a room similar to his, worn curtains and all. Through the tattered lace he saw the figure of a woman walking back and forth. As if Petya had drawn her by his desire, she came to the window and parted the curtains. When she saw Petya, she leaned forward, resting her elbows on the sill and cupping her face in her hands. She had tawny hair and fair skin and a face barely beginning to line. Her smile was genuine. "Hi."

"Hello," said Petya, clearing the constriction in his throat.

The prostitute's brow knitted. "Don't I know you?"

Unable to lie convincingly, Petya said, "Maybe."

"Maybe yes," the prostitute said. "It's been a while. Where you been?"

"In the hills," said Petya. "Five years."

The prostitute whistled. "Without a woman?"

Petya nodded. Against his will, the stirring within him was mounting.

"My sensible side tells me to keep my mouth shut," the prostitute said. "Guys too long in the hills wear me out. I'm no good for anything the rest of the night. My other side says I would love to take the edge off you."

Petya shook his head. "I can't."

The prostitute regarded him without rancor.

"You got troubles, all right." She removed her elbows from the sill. "Oh, well. It don't make any difference." She turned away and said over her shoulder, "If you change your mind, the room number is ten."

· · · ·

Petya was sitting on the bed with his head bowed, staring at the floor, when St. Martin knocked and came in. St. Martin started to tell him it was dinnertime and then stopped short when he saw the silhouette in the window across the alley.

"I should have stayed in the hills," Petya said miserably.

"It's no good," said St. Martin. "That only postpones the testing." He pursed his lips in an effort to recall something. "Once in seminary I read in a book in English some words you should hear. 'The way to the Celestial City lies just through this town, where this lusty fair is kept; and he that will go to the City and yet not go through this town, must needs go out of the world.'" He put his hand on Petya's shoulder. "Do you understand?"

When Petya shook his head, St. Martin said patiently, "No matter. There will come a time when you will."

· · · ·

Except for the bartender washing glasses and an old drunk half asleep at the card table, the saloon was empty. From the common table in the dining room, there was a hum of voices.

The dining room was flooded with electric light that reflected bril-

liantly off the white oilcloth of the common table. The room was long
and narrow, and wooden benches were drawn up on both sides of the
table, which was laden with baskets of French bread, steaming soup
tureens, and bottles of red wine.

The soup had already been served and the men were hunched over
their bowls with elbows planted firmly in front of them. The sounds
of their eating competed with the clatter of dishes and shouting voices
from the kitchen. St. Martin's place was at the head of the table. He was
flanked on either side by two young Basques whose shy manners and
badly fitting broadcloth suits gave away the fact that they had just arrived from the Old Country. They looked and acted like brothers. Petya
glanced at them curiously, wondering how they had managed to elude
the French conscription.

"They were lucky," said a burly Basque next to Petya. "They found a
hole in the frontier." The man had not looked around when Petya came
in. But when Petya turned to him, he looked up to regard him with wry
amusement. He had a round, puckish face and a mouth filled with gold
teeth. Petya stared at him as if he were a ghost.

"Salbador!"

"You are surprised to see me here?"

"I heard you'd gone home."

"I did go home," said Salbador. "The bastards took me in my own
family's house. They were going to shoot me as a deserter."

Petya's mouth formed the question.

"I got away from the French officer who had me," said Salbador.
"I think I hurt him bad. I can never go home now. Ever again." He
surveyed Petya seriously. "Let's get drunk. You and me. Then we'll go
gamble. I feel lucky tonight, but I'm broke already. Can you loan me
some money? You must have a sackful of it saved up."

Petya reached impulsively for his wineglass and took a long drink.
He was shaken. His cheeks felt hot. Looking up, he surprised one of
the young Basques who had been watching him with knitted brows as
if trying to find a key to the perplexity of this new and strange coun-

try. *Be careful,* thought Petya. *Country of wolves.* Without looking at Salbador, Petya shook his head slowly and decisively.

"Oh well . . ." sighed Salbador, and he said no more about gambling or getting drunk on Petya's savings. Petya was amazed. It was so easy and so final, after all, simply to say no to disaster.

· · · · ·

In the privacy of his room, Petya went again to the window. The woman was in her working clothes now, a gauzy dress that even through the curtains revealed her breasts and supple thighs. There was a teetering moment, and then Petya made up his mind. It had to do with tomorrow and the French consul's threat and Laborde's offer, which he was seeing now in all its promise. When he drew down the shade, it had little to do with the friendly prostitute.

18

Below the descending lane, a dense white mist nearly concealed the village of Donibane. Only the lofty church steeple, raising its cross above the sea of mist, indicated there was a village and life below.

When Maitia emerged from the house through the iron-studded portals, she turned and glanced upward out of long habit at the keystone that pronounced that the House of Garat had been built in 1454. She dropped her eyes quickly and ignored the mistake of having looked at the keystone. Her features were frozen in an unseeing, unhearing mask that blotted out the ground in front of the stone fortress of a house. She neither saw nor heard. She was oblivious to the flowers, the flourishing vegetable garden, the clucking hens, and the field beyond, where blonde cows and sheep grazed, and where pigs rooted in the rich soil. The closing of her senses to sights and sounds and memory had begun as she came downstairs carrying a suitcase in each hand. Stirring the embers in the old fireplace with its massive andirons of gray, polished steel, she had made a fire and had her coffee and milk and bread. She had sat on the ancient straight-backed bench, hand-hewn in such a way that the width of its one arm served as a table for plate and cup. Her mother, her grandmother, and generations of Garat women had taken their coffee on that bench. When the nostalgic thought brushed her mind, it died in the numbness there.

When coffee was done, she had washed her cup and plate under the kitchen pump, dried her hands, and slipped on her coat. She forgot altogether to look in at the formal parlor across the foyer, where her mother had first appeared to her as a golden vision.

Ramon, the hired farmhand, was waiting for her outside the great portals. He wore the unchanging dress of the laboring man, a dark blue smock and loosely fitting blue pants. Ramon had not forgotten her instructions. He picked up the two suitcases as if they were weightless and followed behind her to the grilled gateway that separated the house from the country lane.

If I can make it as far as that gate without looking back, I will finish this journey, Maitia told herself. She was successful as far as the gate, but when she began to walk down the lane, she failed. She felt again the calloused hand of her grandfather Garat enclosing her own child hand. She heard the bell-like laughter of her friends and saw through the blur of memory their light-footed figures clad in bright skirts and laced bodices, rope sandals, and many-hued head scarves. As she walked she heard the slapping water of the River Nive flanking one side of the lane and smelled the scents of deep forests of beech and chestnut and berry bushes that flanked the other side.

When Maitia passed beside the moss-covered ramparts of the Citadel and turned into the little graveyard, she could block out the bitterness no longer. She looked down for the last time at her mother's name chiseled into the Garat family tombstone: Jeanne Garat Labadiste.

"Well, Maman, they won," she said.

When it began, it had moved as slowly and as inevitably as a landslide started by a single pebble. She had gone to Bordeaux as she had promised, to care for her mother. Jeanne was already a shadow of her former self. Consumption had ravaged her body. The proud bearing had caved in and the bright willfulness in her eyes was fading to dullness.

To add pain to her pain, the news had arrived that Michel had been trapped in a poison gas attack during the battle at Verdun. He had breathed in the mustard gas and only a miracle could save his lungs. That news was the beginning of the end for Jeanne.

Michel was invalided home, his fine body already beginning to deteriorate. But his will to live was strong, and for an hour or two each day he forced himself to sit up in an armchair close to his mother and sisters. Labadiste did not come to his room.

One afternoon Michel asked for some photographs he had kept from the front. He studied each of them intently and handed them one by one to Maitia and their mother. There was one photograph over which Michel lingered. When he passed it to Maitia, he said, "This is the one man I will never forget."

The photograph was of Michel standing with a group of French soldiers in the rubble of a town that had been shelled. It was taken during a rest leave for the weary soldiers who had been Michel's comrades in arms. There was a French officer standing behind Michel. He was wearing a kepi and had the little moustache that had become *de rigeur* in the French army.

"A few days later," said Michel, "we were back in the trenches. A German gas shell landed in our trench and exploded. I put on my gas mask like the others, but there was a tear in it and I was choking on mustard gas. My captain saw and crawled to me. He pulled away my mask and ripped his own mask off to put it over my nose and mouth. I saw him cover his face with his trench coat, but it was no use. When the all-clear sounded we got up, but he didn't move. My captain was dead."

Maitia handed the photograph to Jeanne. Her mother took it listlessly, held it closer, and turned pale. She sat unmoving a long moment before asking in a voice from the grave, "Your captain, did he know your family name?"

"He did," said Michel. "He was very curious about our family."

"He gave his life for you. He gave his life for me!" whispered Jeanne. And then she had slumped forward in her chair.

Unpredictably, Jeanne decided to die where she had been born, in the House of Garat. It was Maitia who took her home. Jeanne gave no reason for her request and no reason for her demand that she be entombed with her forebears in the graveyard of Donibane.

·   ·   ·   ·

Jean-Baptiste and the mayor, Chasco, had taken advantage of Maitia's absence in Bordeaux. Jeanne was hardly in her grave before Maitia was summoned before the civil magistrate of Donibane. When she entered the courtroom, Chasco regarded her with sly satisfaction in his eyes. Her uncle, Jean-Baptiste, would not look at her.

Clearing his throat, the French magistrate informed Maitia that her grandfather Garat's will had been declared invalid under French law. The testamentary freedom traditionally practiced in the Basque Country was clearly illegal and persisted only because of lax administration of the law. The House of Garat, farmlands and all, was to go to Garat's only surviving heir, Jean-Baptiste Garat. Any claim of Maitia's to her mother's half of the inheritance would be devoid of legal force by reason of the nature of her birth. Out of his generous nature, her uncle had offered to buy her a little shop with living quarters in Donibane where Maitia could live and turn her energies to something like dressmaking, for which he would provide a reasonable sum of money until she could support herself.

Maitia heard the judge out without a word. When he was finished, she said with an anger so cold and chilling that the three men were struck speechless, "You have cheated me."

As for Viktor, her intended husband, that arrangement died stillborn. Viktor vanished as soon as he heard that Maitia had been disinherited. After what had gone before, his disappearance from her life was surprisingly painless.

·   ·   ·   ·

Leaving the graveyard, Maitia walked behind Ramon down the street that led to the depot where she would board the train that would take her to Bordeaux. She knew she could expect nothing when she got there. The only family members she had left—her sisters Madeleine and Marie-Claire—were still living at Labadiste's hotel. Her brother Michel had gone away. Without ever exchanging a word with his father, and feeling strong in his convalescence, he had decided to go to America.

Only a few shopkeepers were up and about when Maitia walked the gauntlet to the railway depot. It would not have mattered to her if they had all been watching. With her back straight and her head held high, she went into the depot and bought her ticket.

There was not a long wait before the little train pulled into the station, steam hissing, its whistle making short, imperative blasts.

Ramon handed Maitia's suitcases to the conductor. Pausing before she mounted the step, Maitia stood on tiptoe and kissed Ramon on the forehead. "Take care of the land, Ramon," she said, brushing away the tears that had welled in his red-rimmed eyes and were rolling down his cheek.

As the train made its noisy departure from Donibane, Maitia sat rigidly straight in her seat, refusing to look either to right or left. When the village was lost to sight, Maitia said, "I never want to see you again."

EPILOGUE

My mother never did.

When the letter from Michel had arrived in Bordeaux, she read it in the stillness of her room and then took it straightaway to Labadiste. It had been sent from California in the United States of America. Michel had gotten as far as San Francisco, where he was living in a little room in a French hotel. He wrote that he had first thought of becoming a sheepherder, like the many other Basques who had gone to America. But he had given up on that idea as his train crossed the cruel Nevada deserts and the mighty mountains of the Sierra. His health was not robust enough to cope with such terrain.

He had gone to a bank looking for polite work, but his command of English was too poor to qualify him. Waiting on tables he would not do, out of pride. His health was deteriorating rapidly, he was almost out of money. What he did not say, but what showed through the finely written lines of French script, was that he had reached the end of his string.

Maitia watched Labadiste's face closely as he read the letter. He was seated in his throne chair, behind the huge wooden desk that was intended to impress his clients. Maitia sat in one of the straight-backed chairs where a generation of young Basques had been informed of their destinations, had been handed train and boat tickets, and had been instructed on the terms of their indenture.

As Labadiste read Michel's words and sensed the pride that rested behind them, he grew progressively more quiet and withdrawn. As he neared the end of the letter, his eyes closed for a moment. Maitia knew that he was overcome with emotions he had never known he could feel.

Labadiste placed the last page of the letter on the pages that had gone before. He sat quietly and then made a decision. In a controlled voice, he told Maitia that she was the only one of the family mature enough and able to go to America and bring back his son. He did not say that his own pride would not permit him to go himself, but Maitia did not need words to understand that. Labadiste would be openhanded with money for passage and expenses in America. Maitia accepted Labadiste's commission without comment.

She went, knowing that she would never come back. She had not deceived herself. Michel was surely dying. He had worn the gray mark of death from the day he had returned home from the army hospital. But she would try to heal the breach between father and son and do her utmost to reunite the two. She felt a twinge of compassion for Labadiste.

· · · ·

Maitia stood on the deck of the ship that was moving through the narrows to New York City. As the sea mists cleared and she saw the Statue of Liberty looming above her, she knew that it signified her emancipation from the stigma she had borne since the night she had been born a Child of the Holy Ghost.

Crossing the immense continent, Maitia followed the same route designated long ago for Labadiste's emigrants to the American West. When she arrived in San Francisco, she learned that for the sake of his lungs, Michel's doctor had advised him to seek a high altitude and dry climate. The highness and dryness were to be found in Reno, on the eastern side of the Sierra Nevada. Michel's note told her he was staying at a little hotel owned by a Basque named St. Martin. Maitia recrossed the mountains to Reno.

St. Martin told her with kindness that Michel was not there anymore, that he had been taken to a hospital called Saint Mary's.

He had collapsed a week after he had come to Reno. With St. Martin as guide, Maitia did not pause to unpack before going to the hospital. She was led to Michel's room and stared in horror at what she saw there. Michel was more cadaver than man. Only his eyes glowing luminously out of the bare bones of his face showed that he was alive at all.

From that day until the day Michel died, Maitia spent her days beside his hospital bed. There was often another visitor in the room, a tall man with the black hair and strong features of the high-country Basques. He was a partner in business with a livestock owner named Laborde and a rising sheepman in his own right. He had been bucked off a horse and sent to hospital. His name was Petya.

During the time that Michel had been alone in the hospital, the doctor and the nurses had asked Petya to interpret for them. Petya had been more than willing, and the instant friendship between Petya and Michel had grown. In Michel's loneliness, Petya's companionship and their ability to communicate in a common language had answered a deep and crying need.

When Michel died, he was buried in a cemetery on the high brow of a hill overlooking Reno. My mother tended his grave until she was unable to. Now, many years later, I go to the cemetery each Memorial Day to place a single rose on the grave of a young French soldier who should have been buried in the earth of his native land, for which he had given his life. "His body is a stranger to America," my father, Petya, once said. And he was right.

·　·　·　·　·

I would not be a proper son of Basques if I did not believe that fate sometimes needs a helping hand to square life's debts. In the case of the smuggler chieftain whose existence had prevented my father from going home long before he did, time evened out the score. When I went with my father on his return to the high Pyrenees near the end of his life, it was to hear a remarkable story. The news could not have been written indelibly in a letter, but it could be told by word of mouth. The smuggler chieftain had made the mistake of getting old. When his lack of judgment began to endanger his band, it became his turn to be catapulted to a bloody death at the bottom of a precipice. "In a way, I'm sorry," my father said when his family told him the story. "I would have liked to kill him myself."

The turn to even out my mother's score came and went without her knowledge. When my older brother Leon was elected governor of our state, the French newspapers made quite a to-do about it. *Son of France! Son of Basques Elected Governor of Nevada!* was splashed in French headlines for a month afterwards. I received the newspapers, read them, and said nothing about them to my mother. Her maiden name was reported as being Labadiste. The village of Donibane had closed up against the outside world to protect its ancient scandal.

When Leon accepted an invitation to go to Paris and then to my mother's natal village, I took my brother aside and spoke to him in confidence. He knew my mother's story now, but he knew nothing about what was happening in the French press. I knew that the mayor of Donibane, very old but still in power, could not avoid participating in the official ceremony when the governor visited his mother's natal home.

"I've never asked you to do me a favor," I told Leon, "but I'm asking you now."

I elicited a promise from him. It was actually a simple promise, and its fulfillment would mean nothing elsewhere in France. But it would mean something in Donibane, where officials and media would be waiting to interview the governor. I coached him, and he memorized in French:

"My mother's name was Maitia Garat, *not* Maitia Labadiste. She was born to Jeanne Garat of the House of Garat of this village. I do not know the name of her father. My mother was born illegitimate. For that innocent crime she was cheated of her rightful inheritance through the manipulations of the mayor of this village. *That* is the real reason she emigrated to America."

Leon kept his promise and I am grateful to him. I am sure that when the mayor has passed on, Leon will be invited again to visit the village of Donibane.

Though my mother said she never wanted to see Donibane and the House of Garat again, it cost her. I know that now. In her last hours, she said, "I want so much to go back and see those beautiful little corners of my valley again. I want you to take me there. I want you to see them with me."

"I've seen them."

My mother shook her head. "Oh, no. You are imagining that from all that I have told you." She dozed, and when she opened her eyes, she said, "My house and my land lie just up this pretty lane that passes beside the ramparts. You will enjoy seeing them as much as I will. Take my hand."